A
TASTY DISH

Regi Jackson-Rotar

PAGE PUBLISHING
Conneaut Lake, PA

First originally published by Page Publishing 2023

ISBN 979-8-88793-238-5 (pbk)
ISBN 979-8-88793-255-2 (digital)

Printed in the United States of America

To the memory of my mother and siblings. I hope I have made you proud. I miss you every day.

To my husband, Tim, for his love, support, and encouragement. To my family, in-laws, out-laws, and everyone in between. To my close circle of friends, who have always had my back and kept me motivated and inspired.

Thank you for helping me find my voice.

Special thanks to Christopher Marzullo for pointing me to the right direction so the details made sense.

A Tasty Dish!

Surround yourself with only people who are going to lift you higher.
—Oprah Winfrey

In any town across the USA, you can always find some little out-of-the-way place to go have a meal; be greeted; be served good food with a smile and at a decent price; and leave the place, feeling satisfied and special. With great service and great food, these places could quickly and easily become your go-to for a quick meal. Finding something better and healthier for you than fast food can be challenging at times. At most places, you'd eat your meal and feel rushed to finish so the waitstaff could turn over the table or booth to have new patrons seated. A Tasty Dish was not the kind of place that would rush you to eat and leave as quickly as possible. They wanted you to enjoy your meal, savor the atmosphere, and feel comfortable lingering for a while.

In the southwestern part of Madison, the capital city of Wisconsin, A Tasty Dish was a chic little bistro owned by five long-time friends. These women were a diverse group; they endearingly referred to themselves as "a mixed bag of nuts." Intelligent, professional, driven, and loyal, each one was a survivor in her own right. These five have been there for one another in the highest of highs and lowest of lows. Chloe, Felicity, Lacey, Raven, and Simone all made sure that A Tasty Dish operated just the way they intended.

A Tasty Dish was smallish by ordinary standards, with ten tables, each seating two to four; eight booths, each seating up to four as well; and six seats at the counter space by the kitchen. Of course, one had the option of placing an order online, calling ahead, or faxing an order for pickup. They accepted all major credit cards, debit, or cash. The business hours were 7:00 a.m. to 6:00 p.m., Monday through Saturday. A Tasty Dish was always closed on Sundays. The busiest hours seemed to be 7:30 a.m. until two in the afternoon. Once the lunch rush was over, there would be a steady flow of traffic slowing down around four-thirty each afternoon. A few folks would stop by on their way home, grabbing dinner or dessert to go. Also, someone from the neighborhood would usually drop in for an early dinner.

The quiche and desserts were served in six-inch pans, offering combinations like shrimp and spinach with onion and cheddar, bacon and broccoli with Pepper Jack or Colby, and ham and Swiss with asparagus. They also offered a vegetable quiche as well as egg-whites-only on request and many other delicious variations.

The weekly soup rotation could remind you of comfort, like a visit to Grandma's kitchen: chili, chicken noodle, broccoli and cheddar, fully loaded baked potato, vegetable, chipotle tortilla, and the neighborhood favorite—chicken and corn chowder. Every Friday, a seafood option would be added to the menu, like New England clam chowder, lobster bisque, or shrimp tomato basil. Felicity and Simone were working on a seafood gumbo recipe to introduce in the fall. All soups were served in a large bowl, with a large corn bread muffin or two biscuits. A heaping garden salad rounded out the modest menu. Each bowl of soup or salad—muffin or biscuits included—would cost you only five bucks.

At A Tasty Dish, the desserts happened to be the specialty of the house, one type being the six-inch pies that started at $5. They offered apple, cherry, blueberry, or blackberry cobbler. In the first week of every month, you could have warm peach cobbler with ice cream. If you wanted a different kind of pie, you could get sweet potato, chocolate silk, lemon meringue, banana, or coconut cream pies for $6. For the crème de la crème cheesecakes, you had a choice, for $8, of New York style topped with fresh fruit of your choice, chocolate mousse, Reese's Peanut Butter, or cookies and cream. The premium cheesecake was $9, and you could have the decadent flavors of Baileys Irish Cream, Kahlua and cream, Crème de menthe, or the RumHaven coconut rum. Monthly cheesecake specials sold out quickly, such as white chocolate raspberry, caramel apple with a warm spiced buttered rum drizzle, or tiramisu. Felicity and Simone were constantly experimenting with recipes. From Thanksgiving through New Year's, the duo created holiday cheesecakes such as peppermint mocha or eggnog with brandy and caramel-pecan topping.

Being within shouting distance of the district police and fire stations didn't hurt either. It should have been intimidating to anyone thinking A Tasty Dish would make an easy target for robbery. They would have been crazy to try. Officers, firemen, EMTs, and plainclothes detectives were stopping by at all hours of the day on duty and off, and law enforcement traffic was pretty steady.

The owners also made a point of taking deposits to the bank at unpredictable times, with never the same person and never the same route. Banking was done before two in the afternoon, and the payroll was processed by direct deposit. A Tasty Dish ran pretty much like a well-oiled machine. Because of their relationship with their employees and the approachable management style by comparison, ATD did not experience a high turnover like most of their competitors.

When the regulars were in the shop, they'd keep a watchful eye out for anything suspicious and became very protective of the quintet. A few of the neighborhood elders would meet each morning, claiming a corner table close to the entrance so they could see the activities, who was coming in, and who was wearing what. Actually, they were quite comical, but their antics were harmless and served as free entertainment for the owners and staff.

A Tasty Dish had its daily customers, yet some folks stopped by only once or twice a week, while others were more random. Management insisted the staff get to know the regulars, from their seating preferences to food choices to idiosyncrasies to occupations. It made recognition as well as conversation easier and made the regular patrons feel special.

The owners did it all in the bistro, which was why they had earned the respect of the staff and the regular patrons. They baked, mixed, prepped food, waited and bussed tables, wash dishes, and worked the front dining room as well as the kitchen. These ladies never asked any staff member to do a task at A Tasty Dish they wouldn't roll up their sleeves up and do themselves. There was always at least one owner present from opening to closing. You could count on it!

They had bought the office space adjoining the café and knocked down the wall to accommodate waiting patrons, especially on Saturdays. The work schedule was staggered, but on Saturdays, it was all hands on deck. Simone would be the first to arrive to meet Walker and Diego, who kept order in the kitchen. Walker was like a stand-up comic. Simone would make coffee while setting the televisions out front to CNN, stocking the display case up front, putting cash in the registers, and making sure the place was customer-ready until Kennedy, the café manager, arrived at seven. Raven and Chloe would usually come in by ten to get ready for the lunch rush with their mix of '70s or '80s music piped in.

They would mix and mingle with customers as they worked. Felicity would bounce in half an hour after that, full of energy as the force she could be, greeted by customers like a celebrity. Lacey would show up at eleven, always distracted by some drama in her home. By noon every Saturday, A Tasty Dish would be in full swing for the day, yet behind-the-scenes prep would already be started for the following week.

The café started as a passing idea, and it skyrocketed from there. A few months later, they received an offer too good to pass up, now known as Your Just-Desserts. It was off the capital-square area of the city, with hours from ten to four from Mondays through Fridays and nine to three on Saturdays. You could pick up a six- or twelve-inch pie or cheesecake to go. At the grand opening, the samples spoke for themselves, and the fierce five knew that business would be great!

Meanwhile, things were always hectic to the east in Sun Prairie, at Tasty Express—a smaller version of A Tasty Dish main café with a less extensive menu that had more sandwiches, salads, and basic desserts. The hours at the Express were Monday through Saturday, ten to six. Here, it was standing room only from eleven to three-thirty, also known as the SP lunch rush.

Whenever either of the locations was short-staffed, Chloe, Raven, and Simone's connections in several local employment agencies came in handy, and whenever the girls Tallulah, Reese, Dakota, and Mia came home from college, they were more than happy to pitch in and earn some spending money in their pockets for when they went back to school.

These young ladies learned from their mothers early the value of hard work and honesty. They started helping out as soon as they were ready—first bussing tables, tidying up small spills, washing dishes, and then moving up to serving water. Eventually, they could fill in for any staff member whenever there was a need, and they did so with no complaints. Some of the regular neighborhood patrons had watched them grow into beautiful, spirited young adults who had very bright futures ahead of them.

The three business entities kept the quintet very busy, very happy, and very successful!

✦

A Tasty Dish Family

People inspire you, or they drain. Pick them wisely.
—Hans F. Hansen

Working at A Tasty Dish felt comfortable. It felt good to work there; you were appreciated and respected. The owners took pride in their employees. Each of them understood that if you treated people well, you'd always have loyal, dedicated people working for you. Everyone cheered for the continued success of this small business, from staff to customers and residents in the neighborhood. This was a feel-good place!

Anika, a freshman at the university, worked on Tuesday, Thursday, and Friday evenings from 4:00 p.m. to 6:30 p.m. and every Saturday from 12:00 p.m. to 6:30 p.m. She was polite, quiet, and kind and always smiled, but she was very serious. If you tried to get too close, she would stiffen up and shut down. After a few months at the café, Simone was able to get her to open up. She had that maternal charm. Anika didn't even realize what was happening, and Simone never pressed her. But their relationship grew stronger after that, and for the first time in her short life, the young woman knew what it felt like to trust someone. And it felt good.

Anika came from Chicago. She wanted to study medicine, and her only way out of a dysfunctional household was to work as hard as she could in school. She was able to secure a full scholarship to the University of Wisconsin in Madison. Anika graduated from high school as valedictorian with honors and accolades, but it didn't matter to her family. They were all too busy with their pettiness and perceived dramas to be bothered to attend the graduation ceremony of their eldest daughter. When Chloe went to hug Anika on her birthday, she could sense that the girl was not used to being hugged or shown any affection, for that matter.

Anika had a bare-bones wardrobe and was obsessed with keeping everything she owned clean. She kept her long curly blond hair in a ponytail or a French braid. When Christmas rolled around, Anika offered to work extra shifts for others. She was always determined not to return to Chicago for the holidays. She'd rather stay in the dorm practically alone with microwave pizza than endure the pain of going home. When Simone realized this, she insisted Anika spend the holidays at her home. Her daughter Tallulah would be home from college as well as Reese, Dakota, and Mia. She knew the girls would definitely get along and be welcoming toward Anika. In fact, Simone believed this would be just the thing she needed to get her out of her shell.

The evening hostess and cashier, Delaney, affectionately nicknamed Little D by regular customers, was a junior in high school, an honor student, a varsity cheerleader, and a slight prankster by nature. Delaney was always very helpful around the café. She worked after school on Mondays and Wednesdays from 4:00 p.m. to 6:30 p.m., offering assistance whenever it was needed in the café. On Saturdays, she was at A Tasty Dish from 2:00 p.m. to 6:30 p.m. She was quick to greet and seat. Everyone really liked the sweet young lady who was a force of positive energy in a very small package.

Delaney had early aspirations of becoming a lawyer. She first started talking about it as early as middle school. That was when she started displaying a talent for debating. By high school, she was unstoppable, winning local, regional, and state debates. In her sophomore year, Delaney made her national debut. Every Tuesday, she had mock trials at school as part of an extracurricular activity. Fourteen honor students from all over the city had a chance to play lawyer with fictional cases—a defense, a prosecutor, and some witnesses. And acting as judge was the law professor who volunteered his time to be part of this program at one of the local high schools and mentor students seriously interested in pursuing a career in law. Whichever side she was on, Delaney was usually a rock star; she always did her homework and came prepared to win.

Diego assisted Walker in the kitchen. He wore many hats, and like everyone else, he did a bit of everything at ATD. Plus, he took over whenever Walker was not around. He worked part-time as a security guard at the university to earn enough to help keep his daughters in private school. Diego was married to Gracie and was a proud father to Sasha, eight years old, and Skye, six.

At A Tasty Dish, the owners led by example. The work ethic was strong, and the expectations were high. Any employee who felt they were too good to rinse dishes, load the dishwasher, or help take out garbage didn't last long.

The place was managed well. Raven handled all human resources and personnel matters while Chloe processed the data for the payroll company and worked the business office. Lacey handled all maintenance, facility, and equipment functions and kept close contact with the janitorial service. Felicity worked together with Simone on menu planning, ordering, and making sure Walker and Diego had all the recipes and ingredients they needed. All five ladies contributed to marketing campaigns and strategies.

Valencia opened the café and waited tables from Monday through Friday, 6:30 a.m. to 1:00 p.m., with rotating Saturday afternoons. She was overwhelming in stature at 5'11", with an uncommonly soft voice, a sweet smile, and beautiful long red hair, yet never a strand was out of place. Valencia had been a stay-at-home mom, but now her kids were in high school. She was enjoying the extra money she was earning at A Tasty Dish, and the tips were an added bonus! Her husband, Chase, co-owned an architectural firm with Sebastian, Felicity's spouse, and Chase was great about pitching in and helping Valencia run the house.

Emme waited tables and had the closing responsibilities. She worked from 11:30 a.m. to 6:30 p.m. from Monday through Friday and shared the rotating Saturday afternoons with Valencia. She was all of 5'2", with the graceful ability to deliver three plates at once without missing a step or bumping into anyone, all while seeming to move to music no one else heard! *Sassy* pretty much described her, and she kept the regulars on their toes with her quick wit. After a contentious divorce, Emme was still a hopeless romantic, but she always joked about finding "Mr. Right about Now."

Jourdana only worked on Saturdays from 6:30 a.m. until 1:00 p.m., but she stayed later to help out if it was really busy and would sometimes fill in for Valencia or Emme, which meant one of the owners would help fill in her shift. Jourdana was a kept woman. Her job at A Tasty Dish gave her a little time out on her own and some pocket change, and it kept things interesting. She was an artist; and her partner, Chelsea, was a pretty ruthless financial analyst with a three-figure salary. Jourdana's paintings were not drawing the gallery and art-community attention she'd hoped, but Chelsea didn't care. If painting kept her "baby girl" happy, then so be it. Chelsea was willing to rent gallery space if that was what Jourdana wanted.

Walker was the kitchen manager. His full name was Steven Dexter Walker. He had been called Walker since early childhood and had missed his calling as a stand-up comedian. He was not at all crass, just comical and very animated. There was a belief that Walker never met a stranger and could possibly be one of the nicest guys you've ever met. A retired Marine who served his country by finishing out his twenty-year career in Afghanistan, Walker was just glad to have that chapter of his life in the rear-view mirror. His wife, Constance, had passed away three years earlier from lung cancer. The love of his life was a strong, stoic woman but not strong enough to give up cigarettes even after her diagnosis. She had been in a three-year remission after surgery, but the cancer returned with a fury. She declined rapidly after that and was still smoking. They never had children but spoiled any kid they knew.

Just Regular Folks

*The past is your lesson. The present is your
gift. The future is your motivation.*

—Unknown

The regulars at A Tasty Dish consisted of a varied collection of mixed nuts. There were people from the neighborhood who would stop by every day for coffee, quiche, or something sweet to eat for breakfast to go along with their gossip. Then there were others on their way to work and even some on their way home from an overnight shift. Some called in an order for pickup, while others enjoyed the break from rush-hour traffic from point A to point B.

One daily patron who stopped in on his way to the office was Jude, a lawyer high up in the food chain. He was a partner at his firm who was very good-looking, very well dressed in his Valentino suits, and always smelled so good that it could be almost intoxicating, along with his smooth and fast talking. Jude flirted with all the women at A Tasty Dish, from staff to owners as well as customers. If you smiled or acknowledged him in any way, that was just the invitation he needed. He was a really pretty boy who thought he was God's gift to women. Jude believed every woman needed and wanted his attention, as insincere and obnoxious as it was.

Fifty percent of the time, Jude did not wear his wedding band, and you could easily see the ring shadow. He came in from Monday through Friday at 8:15 a.m. You could almost set your watch by his arrival, and what an entrance he made. He'd sit in a booth if one was available, then he'd have coffee and a muffin or quiche, sometimes just toast. But he tipped extremely well. On Fridays, Jude would have his coffee and make small talk with regulars while the server packed up his special weekly standing order, which was always one of the signature desserts: a perfectly boxed and bowed Bailey's Irish Cream, Kahlua and cream, or any of the other exclusives.

A Tasty Dish's colors were black, white, and pink. Every to-go box was a variety of this color combination: solid black, black-and-white stripes, or black-and-white polka dots. All were tied and bowed with a pink satin ribbon. For Jude, it was the same every week: a solid-black box with a pink ribbon. And once, he even criticized the ribbon-cutting skills of Valencia until Simone intervened. Sir Jude, as the owners referred to him, had visited several times on a Saturday, and a few times he was accompanied by his wife, Scarlet.

Jude's wife was a beautiful smartly dressed woman who, even on a weekend, looked like she was waiting to pose for a cover photo shoot for *Town & Country* magazine. There were no children for this couple… Jude did not want her to "get all big and bloated." The charmer that he was, Scarlet knew exactly what she had signed up for!

Any man would have been proud to have Scarlet as his wife and treated her well, for she was the total package of beauty, brains, and personality. To Jude, she was his trophy—something to be shown off and represent *his* success. His infidelity was a different matter altogether, and the type of women involved in Jude's affairs could not have been more opposite of Scarlet. They were not intelligent; they lacked class, and three to five minutes in conversation with any one of them left no doubt that they didn't do well in the academic world.

These women were pretty but of very little depth. The one common thread among them was that they all finished high school with no real ambition and shared dreams of being taken care of—being a kept woman! They were foolish enough to be used by men like Jude. The owners believed Scarlet had to be aware of her husband's indiscretions. Scarlet, as it turned out, was a diabetic. So who were those weekly perfectly packaged desserts for?

Marlowe was a nurse who would stop by every morning during the week, after her night shift at University Hospital ended. She usually sat at a table and read the local newspaper, although there were some mornings when she was just too tired and would call ahead to place her order for pickup. While dining in, Marlowe would keep to herself. She was friendly toward everyone, just extremely shy and usually exhausted after a night on the floor in palliative care. It was emotionally draining for her, but she was a great comfort to families that were losing loved ones soon. The best they could do on her floor was keep patients as comfortable as possible until they passed on. Marlowe was slightly overweight, wore glasses, and wore no makeup at all. Yet there was an approachable warmth about her.

Hope, a retired middle school principal, would walk to A Tasty Dish every morning at seven-thirty with a newspaper in hand. She'd claim a table near the front entrance for the other neighborhood regulars. Hope was outgoing and opinionated, which was a fact she was always more than willing to share with others. You never had to guess or wonder where she stood on any issue. Three days a week and on Saturdays, she would return at 4:30 p.m. for a light dinner. From ten in the morning to three in the afternoon during the week, her days were filled with tutoring at one of the middle schools.

Hope was passionate about turning students who were too often categorized as negative statistics into students starving to learn and with a bright future ahead of them. She could work magic with students one-on-one because of her positive attitude and her sense of humor. Hope made it fun by showing the kids how smart they really were; and she knew that all each of them needed and wanted was for somebody, anybody, to believe in them.

Regulars also included uniformed police officers. There was Terrence, a by-the-book type who had been on the force for ten years, and his partner, Roxanne, a no-nonsense, originally-from-Texas bleached blond who loved her spray tan about as much as the fact that she was one of the city's first female officers. There was also Officer Dennison, otherwise known as Denny, who was down-to-earth, had great people skills, and was always tasked with the rookies. At present, Denny was partnered with everybody's favorite rookie,

Alec, who wanted to move up rapidly and was now getting a serious taste of having to put in the work first. Alec was learning the hard way that regardless of whomever you're related to, you still have to work your way up and that good looks and connections don't matter.

The café also had routine visits from the firehouse across the street from the police station. There was Captain Jake Santana (or Salt, as everyone referred to him) and Lieutenants Jayden Fletcher and Roman Riley, both with model-good looks, which made most people believe it was a prerequisite to join the fire department). Zoey, a firefighter, and Carson, a paramedic, met at the café before every shift for breakfast along with their free coffee to wash it down. Jasmine, the office manager, would call in an order for the firehouse staff. Oliver, her assistant, would pick the order up on his way to work.

Chloe

*A friend is someone who knows the song in our heart and can
sing it back to you when you have forgotten the words.*

—Unknown

Chloe had been married to Andre for over twenty-five years.
They were college sweethearts and wed right after graduation. Chloe graduated with a degree in business administra-
tion, while Andre finished with an advanced degree in computer science. The two of them put their higher education to use immediately,
but both had ambitions of one day owning their own businesses.

Together they were a great couple. Andre stood at 6'2" and had
solid-blue eyes and dark-blond hair with a few gray strands peeking
through, compared to Chloe's 5'4" stature and medium-length bob
of straight auburn hair, which accentuated beautiful big brown eyes.

The couple had a daughter, Dakota, who, at twenty-one years old,
had just graduated from nursing school with honors at the University of
Arizona in Tucson. It had been a long four years, and the very health-con-
scientious young woman with a personality like a firecracker had already
secured a position in a Madison hospital. The family was also busy planning Dakota's wedding, which would be a few months later.

The family went on adventures every summer: road trips to
national parks, camping out, hiking, rafting, biking, and seeing the
incredible sights this country had to offer. But mostly it was about
being a family and enjoying life to its fullest.

When the time came for Dakota to leave for college, Chloe took
it hard, very hard! The two were very close. Even though Dakota was

"""

a smart, driven, and independent young lady, Chloe was emotionally drained. She cried plenty the first couple of weeks. Raven assured her, "It does get easier." With the help of Skype, FaceTime, and all other avenues of communication, Chloe was comforted. What helped the most was seeing Dakota being so busy and so positive and doing so well on her own, which made her mother proud.

When Dakota was younger, Chloe was involved in a bad car crash after one of those Wisconsin snowstorms turned to rain and iced everything over. She was on her way home from work. The other driver, traveling way too fast, didn't see the red light and, in midintersection, hit his brakes. His car fishtailed and skidded right into Chloe's driver's side. It was a horrific crash. The other driver, stunned and without so much as a scratch, managed to stumble out of his car. Chloe's vehicle, practically mangled beyond recognition, sat in the middle of the street, with the driver's side door smashed almost completely in. Chloe wasn't able to move. There was only stillness and silence.

Fortunately, a woman walking her dog witnessed the impact; she had stopped at the corner to videotape her small pooch jumping on mini mounds of snow. When she hit Play Back, she realized she had caught the other driver running the red light while texting, and she assumed that he was probably inebriated. This witness caught the driver clearly distracted, speeding, and running a red light on an icy road in the middle of winter.

The witness called 911 to report the crash. She told them, "The vehicle that has been struck has the female driver pinned in her car, and the other driver is trying to leave the scene! But I have all of his vehicle info on my phone."

Police were immediately dispatched, and fire and rescue arrived a few minutes later. The fire team took one look at Chloe's car and knew it would be a difficult task to get her extracted from the vehicle. The emergency medical team took to the task of keeping Chloe calm until they could get her out. She was not in hysterics, but it was just a matter of time before she'd realize the severity of her situation.

The driver's side door had been pushed all the way to the rear door and was now just a mangled heap. The emergency and fire crew had to cut the car around Chloe to free her. The EMTs had to call a medivac life flight for transport to the trauma center.

Even though she was in shock, the physicians on duty were amazed at how lucky Chloe was to have survived an impact like that. She was alive, but everything below the waist looked bad. Her legs were very badly damaged, and they knew they would need to perform several emergency surgeries to try to save each leg.

After the first four surgeries, Chloe dug her heels in for months of physical and occupational therapy along with plenty of tears and emotional outbursts. After all was said and done, once she had learned to walk again, Chloe started slow, first by walking at the gym at physical therapy every day to strengthen her legs and get out of the house. After working up to jogging, Chloe started running, and that was all she wrote. She challenged herself by taking on a five-kilometer run, which she finished. Her friends were there to support and celebrate. After that, it was ten-kilometer runs, and you didn't want to be the one standing between her and any goal she had set.

Her friends helped Chloe and Andre get through that awful time. They helped with shuttling Dakota to school and whatever extracurricular activities she was involved in. For the months Chloe was laid up, her crew took turns bringing meals over to the family, helping with laundry, and helping with grocery shopping, and one of them would visit every other day. Because that's what friends do!

Chloe and Andre got through that. They were so grateful for the help that when she was back in action, the family honored their friends with an appreciation dinner in their home. Chloe baked her special lasagna—one with Italian sausage and one vegetable (the women's favorite) with mushrooms, zucchini, spinach, and tomatoes. Raven brought a chopped salad with her homemade raspberry dressing. Felicity furnished three different cheesecakes: blueberry, strawberry, and cookies and cream. Lacey provided three appetizer trays: crudités, artichoke, and spinach dip with strips of French bread plus a platter of fried ravioli and stuffed mushrooms. Simone made lemonade for the kids and brought a batch of her sangria, which she made for the ladies, and the guys were all happy with her choice of various imported beers. This was how the group celebrated their milestones!

Felicity

Friends are the people who make you smile
brighter, laugh louder, and live better.

—Unknown

Felicity and Sebastian had been college sweethearts as well; she was a New Yorker through and through! When you walked into any room, Felicity was the first to approach and greet you. She was a positive force with a disarming smile and flawless skin. She was tall and slim with curves and had a head full of jet-black curls down her back. At 5'11", Felicity was the tallest in this quintet and a standout in any crowd.

The couple married two years after Felicity graduated from NYU and Sebastian from MIT. The distance during those years was never an issue. They were sweet together, and even after years of marriage, they still flirted with each other and kept their date nights twice a month, and Felicity's face would light up whenever she spoke of Sebastian. When the guys would gently tease one another about their wives, Sebastian would usually maintain an innocent boyish grin as his eyes lit up with pride.

Mia, the couple's daughter, could have easily passed for a young Felicity, with the exception of her hair. Mia loved keeping her hair short; she felt it was so much easier to fit into her daily routine, which usually involved running or swimming, and even the Midwest winters didn't stop her. Mia knew the location of most indoor running tracks in the area as well as the warm-water pools. She spent plenty of time at Simone's, doing laps in their pool with their daughter, Tallulah.

Mia was in her sophomore year at FIT (the Fashion Institute of Technology) in New York City, with a full scholarship after winning first place in a national contest for aspiring designers between the ages of fifteen to seventeen. Mia was a junior and sixteen when she won this prestigious award for students with serious, recognizable talent. Always a great student who worked hard at everything, from babysitting to volunteer programs, she also had a part-time job at an exclusive boutique as a personal shopping assistant and still found time to have a little fun. In her last year in high school, Mia already had an impressive résumé.

Felicity and Sebastian adapted to their empty nest quite well. Work at the growing architectural firm where he was one of two owners kept Sebastian very busy. Felicity worked her scheduled rotations at the café, and one of her biggest responsibilities was working with Simone on weekly menus and specials, making sure Walker and Diego had all recipes for the following week so they could place their order for supplies and ingredients by noon on Tuesday so that on Saturday, the kitchen duo would be able to prep everything for the following week.

Felicity handled branding for ATD—labels, special to-go packaging, black-and-white and pink boxes, ribbons, business cards, stationery, and note cards. As part of the community, the women took turns representing A Tasty Dish at all various city functions; there were always two owners in attendance.

When Mia was a freshman in high school, Felicity's world came crashing down around her. She went in for her annual mammogram. An exam that should have taken forty minutes took three hours. After second and third opinions, the doctors confirmed the results. This was not good news for Felicity or her family. After all necessary tests were performed, Felicity was diagnosed with breast cancer and would need a radical mastectomy very soon.

Everything happened so fast, and no one was surprised when Sebastian took over. His priority, as always, was to his family, and this was so now more than ever. He would do his job at the office with the dedication and professionalism he was known for, but he decided that at this time, he did not need to be available to clients 24-7. The wining and dining could be left to Chase, who assured Sebastian, "Take all the time you need. Our clients more than understand and are very supportive. We've spoiled them. They will not jump ship!"

Felicity's surgery to remove her breasts was scheduled for two weeks. She remained in good spirits, but those closest to her could tell she was scared. Felicity had every right to be frightened; she had lost her mother to the same disease when she was just a girl. Most could see past the mask of bravery she tried to wear.

Sebastian had called the school on Friday and spoken to the attendance office to have Mia excused for the day on Monday. His daughter had made it abundantly clear during the previous week that she wanted to be at the hospital: "Dad, there is no way I'm going to school on Monday! I don't care how early we have to be at the hospital. I'm going too, so just make the phone call now."

The doctors operated early on Monday morning, and by that afternoon, after a few hours in recovery, Felicity was in her own hospital room, drowsy but aware that her family was by her side. That first day was hard, as the pain medications did what they were supposed to. By the next morning, Felicity was all smiles when the doctor told her she'd be able to eat solid food for lunch. She laughed and said, "Oh thank God, I was starting to worry!"

After six days, Felicity was discharged from the hospital. The three of them knew they had the full support of their friends, and they joined Gilda's Club immediately. It made a big difference for all of them. That became a big part of the weekly routine. Every Tuesday night, it was dinner at the club for patients and their families, and after dinner, the support group began their discussions. Felicity had four to five weeks before chemotherapy started. She was very tired, but the oncologist gave her kudos for having such a great attitude and always having that gorgeous smile. Felicity had shown just how strong she really was.

Mia became an amazing right hand to her father. Every evening, Sebastian arrived home to find his daughter had completed most of her homework, started dinner, and tidied up the kitchen, all while keeping

Felicity entertained as she sat at the breakfast counter, watching her daughter wondering how she was such a lucky woman. Sebastian and Mia were committed to Felicity's recovery as much as she was.

Every Wednesday, Felicity was taken in for chemo, and when that was over, she was exhausted and weak for the rest of the day.

Of course, Chloe, Raven, Lacey, and Simone were present to help out in any way they could. They brought new dishes of comfort food for meals each week after chemo, they secured a rotation of friends to assist Sebastian in getting Felicity to and from appointments, and they sat with her during outpatient chemo when he or Mia was not available as well as helped her around the house and visited when she was up to it. Simone had ordered five special pink T-shirts made with the words "My best friends are the sisters I hand-picked for myself."

After months of chemotherapy, Felicity had a break. It was five weeks later that she started her radiation treatments. Three times a week, for six weeks, she endured the routine. She stayed positive and joked, "It seems to take longer, getting undressed before and dressed after, than the actual treatment. How is that even possible?" Then she would let out one of her signature giggles.

Felicity was mending rapidly; her conquering spirit served her well. Her strength slowly returned just as radiation was winding down. She had mild side effects but nothing as devastating as what they had prepared her to expect. Little by little, she was ready to live her life on her own terms and take on the world again!

The timing couldn't have been more fitting, cabin fever was starting to set in, therefore driving Sebastian and Mia a little crazy. As they celebrated knowing Felicity was a survivor, each of them breathed a deep sigh of relief, in realizing things were back to normal, but mostly how much the three of them loved and valued each other.

When Felicity returned to A Tasty Dish, she didn't miss a beat. Driven, she picked up where she left off. All the regular patrons were in attendance for lunch on Saturday to welcome her back. The five women all wore the special T-shirts Simone had bought as Sebastian, Andre, Dietrich, and Drake took over a booth back by the kitchen. It was a real celebration, and all was right with the world!

Kennedy

*Getting over a painful experience is much like crossing monkey
bars. You have to let go at some point in order to move forward.*
—C. S. Lewis

Kennedy had been a part of Simone's life since she was a teenager. She was in high demand as a babysitter in Tucson, Arizona. Late one Saturday morning, she decided to walk her young charges to the park. Simone sat on the grass, reading political science homework as the kids played on the swings. On a picnic table nearby, sitting alone, a boy about six years old had his head on the table, in tears.

Simone assumed he was probably lost. She approached carefully so as not to startle him. His face was red as he looked up to answer her when she asked, "Are you all right?" He wiped his face with dirty hands and said, "Yes, I'm okay, but my tummy hurts a little." The boy hesitantly stood up and held out his hand to shake Simone's. She could see he had been sitting on a folded blanket. There was a beat-up Flintstones lunch box next to it.

"My name is Kennedy. Pleased to meet you."

Simone took the dirty little hand, secretly wishing she could take him to the bathroom and wash his face and hands. "Hi, Kennedy. My name is Simone. It's nice to meet you too." Not wanting to give the boy the third degree, however, the always-curious teenager wondered what was he doing here, so young and so alone.

Simone was very aware of the three siblings playing on the swings and having a grand time, oblivious to the world outside the swings. They knew they were safe with Simone, and the little boy she was talking to was certainly no threat. She couldn't stand it anymore. She had to know. "Kennedy, do you live around here?"

He tried to flatten the wrinkles in his shirt as he made direct eye contact with her. "Uh-huh, on Drucker Street, but Mama dropped me off here yesterday after we had dinner at McDonald's. Now we're playing a game. That's how come I gotta wait here."

Simone gasped at the thought that this boy had spent the night in the park alone. What kind of game was his mother playing? Her heart sank as she realized that this boy's mother was more than likely not coming back! The youngest of three, Simone questioned every-thing and was taught early on that if it didn't make sense, something was probably not right in any situation. Right and fair were not the same thing. She had been sitting, quizzing Kennedy for an hour; and it was time to get the kids back to her house to have lunch, read a story, and wind them down before their mother picked them up. Although, their mother could be counted on to be late, especially if she was shopping.

Simone had to insist that Kennedy accompany them to her home in the age before cell phones and pagers. "We can call your mama from our house. We are just moving the game to my house. It'll be fun, really!" But Kennedy insisted he had to wait for his mother to return, or she might be mad at him.

Dahlia, Simone's mother, was a pediatric nurse, and she would know just what to do. With a little more prodding from the children, Kennedy happily joined the group. As the youngsters went skipping, marching, and hopping, he chatted and giggled with the two boys and joined them in teasing their own sister about how "yucky" girls were.

When they arrived at Simone's house, Dahlia helped Simone prepare lunch for the youngsters. It was the perfect time to explain how she met Kennedy in the park. The children were all washing up for lunch. Brennan, Bronson, and Brooklyn all knew the drill, and Kennedy watched them closely. When the laughter got too loud in the bathroom, Dahlia went to check in. As each kid held out their lit-tle hands, she inspected them closely and smiled. Noticing Kennedy's tear- and dirt-stained face, she went into the linen closet, took out a washcloth, wet it with warm water, and gently wiped his face and neck. She discreetly checked him for bruising, burns, or anything that would indicate child abuse. Kennedy smiled at her in appreciation, and Dahlia saw the deepest blue eyes she had ever seen.

Once the kids were settled at the breakfast nook with grilled cheese, Tater Tots, apple slices, and juice, Simone was able to finally look inside the lunch box Kennedy had guarded so closely. She told her mother the label inside read "Kennedy Parker." Dahlia was on the phone with the non-emergency police line as well as CPS. A thoroughly entertained Kennedy was unaware of the tense expressions of Simone and her mother as they waited for a response. Any kind of news was better than not knowing. Kennedy must have been some kind of hungry; he asked for seconds of everything, and, of course, he seemed surprised when he got it!

Was he lost? Did he wander away from home? Was he telling the truth about being dropped off at the park? There were more questions than answers as Dahlia paced back and forth by the phone. They each held their breath, actually hoping that the three siblings would be picked up before the police showed up, if they were coming. You never want to arrive at the babysitter's house to pick up your children and see a police car parked in the driveway. Although they could explain, Simone had done the right thing—not leaving an abandoned child at the park.

Bree Carlizi arrived to pick up her troop twenty minutes late as usual and, in only Bree style, showed no concern for the extra child in the mix of things. She probably assumed it was another *rug rat* being looked after by Simone. Yes, *rug rats, ankle biters*, and *crumb snatchers* are exactly how Bree referred to kids in general. The only reason she had three children herself? It was in the prenuptial agreement when she, a gold digger by nature, married Orlando Carlizi, a man from one of the wealthiest families in the area. Bree spent most of her days striving hard to be the best-dressed woman anywhere! Bree didn't have a job, and during the week, her children were looked after by a nanny. She wanted to ship them off to boarding school when they were old enough, but Orlando was not allowing that.

As the kids were being loaded into the car with the assistance of Simone, their hugs were warm, and their giggles hung in the air. They loved their time with Simone, and it always ended too soon. The Mercedes was out of sight when one police vehicle followed closely by a sedan drove into the circular driveway.

With Kennedy down in the den for some TV time, they spoke with Simone first. She was able to give an account of what occurred at the park. As always, she was detailed-oriented and took notes on everything. She had observed what Kennedy did as well as what he said. The officer told Dahlia that they discovered a Parker residing on Drucker. But the house was vacant, and all research including speaking with the owner of the property showed no forwarding address. According to the owner, Amanda Parker had never indicated that she would be vacating the premises.

Officer Liam Wainright, accompanied by social worker Eden Harper, followed Dahlia and Simone through the house to the den. Kennedy was sprawled on the floor, watching *Batman*. He sat up when they entered the room, and from the look on his face, one could say that the young boy thought he was in trouble when he saw Wainright in uniform. The officer introduced himself and the social worker as both squatted to eye level with Kennedy, who was now on his feet.

The one thing about Kennedy that everyone observed immediately when they met him was how extremely polite and well-mannered he was. He even addressed Simone as *Miss Simone*.

The policeman and the social worker spoke softly to him, and Kennedy began to relax, realizing he wasn't in trouble. Every time he was asked a question, he looked quizzically at Dahlia, who walked over and sat on the floor. She signaled for him to sit next to her. As she put her arm around the boy, his expression changed. The two visitors along with Simone sat on the floor as well. They all saw a connection when Kennedy looked up at Dahlia and smiled as she said, "We all want to help. You can tell these nice people anything that may help us so you and you and your mother can finish your game."

They needed to have Kennedy placed in emergency foster care until the situation could be sorted out. Kennedy pulled on Dahlia's shirt, then whispered in her ear. But for a six-year-old, his whispers were overheard: "Miss Dahlia, how come I can't stay here with you until Mama comes back?" Why indeed? After her husband, Jackson Grant Jr., was killed in Vietnam when his team's helicopter was shot down and there were no survivors, Dahlia was devastated but tried to be strong for her children.

The home had been certified by the state for years now and had seen its share of foster kids come and go. Liam Wainright and Eden Harper both smiled. "Kennedy, I think that's a perfect idea! Boy, you're a smart young man." The boy beamed with a smile from ear to ear.

Wainright thought with a smirk that by having Kennedy at Dahlia's, there was only going to be half of the paperwork to fill out for the incident report. They knew Kennedy was safe, in good hands, and in a great environment. Upon leaving, they both assured Dahlia that they would have all information on Kennedy forwarded to her within twenty-four hours to make an attempt at keeping his young life from being turned upside down—school records, medical records, any CPS reports, everything.

After Wainright and Harper left, Dahlia looked at her watch. They needed to get this boy cleaned up and settled. The three pairs of dingy underpants in his lunchbox weren't going to work. She grabbed her purse and car keys and shouted laughingly to Simone and Kennedy, "Last one to the car is a rotten egg!" Simone purposely let the little boy run in front of her, and he laughed at his victory as he climbed into the back seat of the car. With the sun over the mountains in the west, the trio traveled to Sears at the mall, to the boy's department.

Underwear, T-shirts, shirts and pants for school, shoes, socks, pajamas and, of course, something for church—Dahlia had Kennedy try on each piece to allow the slightest room for growth. He even picked some of the pieces on his own, and he was thrilled because "That's the first time I ever got to pick out my own stuff!" Amanda had always picked his clothes: long pants, long-sleeve plaid shirts, white socks, and loafers. Anything else was "Satan's outfits," she told her son.

Simone assured him, "We'll do it this way until your mother comes back. We'll go to church tomorrow, and you'll have so much fun." They stopped for dinner at TGI Friday's, one of Simone's favorite places. When they returned home, Simone put all of Kennedy's new clothes in the wash while Dahlia ran his bath. While soaking in Mr. Bubble and warm water, she shampooed and rinsed his hair, then cleaned his ears with a Q-tip. Dahlia wasn't surprised that it took six Q-tips to get his ears really clean, then she left him to clean the rest of his body. When he was done, he dried himself off as best he could and put on the new bathrobe that Simone had just taken from the dryer. It felt good on his skin, and he thought it smelled wonderful.

Dahlia brought in his pajamas and said, "We'll watch a movie before bedtime. You can choose." As she saw the dirt ring in the bathtub, she thought that it was as if he had been working in the field all day. It seemed that his little body had not seen a good scrubbing in a while. Simone was busy putting everything away in his room. *His room,* she thought and smiled to herself. No one knew how long Kennedy would be in Dahlia's care. That was up to Amanda Parker, the social workers, and the foster care system.

Sunday after service, and attendance at the church picnic the three musketeers would scout for school supplies and, according to Kennedy, a new lunchbox. Dahlia and Simone were very careful not to bad-mouth Amanda Parker; no good would come from that. Dahlia's two older children were adults and on their own. Paloma lived in San Diego with her husband, and Jackson Grant III worked for the US Geological Survey. When they received the news about Kennedy, both were ecstatic and couldn't wait to meet him.

While shopping for the school supplies he needed, an exhausted Kennedy was ready for bath and bed when they returned to the Grant home. This night, even though he played hard at the picnic, there was hardly any dirt residue in the bathtub like the night before. Monday morning came with no drama. Dahlia made breakfast burritos for everyone with egg whites, turkey sausage, cheese, potatoes, and onions. Kennedy had one and a half as he explained how he had never had anything like that. Breakfast was always cold cereal.

Simone made his lunch: a turkey sandwich, an apple, cookies, chips, and a small carton of chocolate milk.

Simone had the luxury of driving her small car to school since Dahlia had to go to the office with Kennedy to talk to the principal, the school nurse, and his teacher as well as temporarily change his emergency contact information.

Months passed, and no one ever heard from Amanda Parker. Kennedy thrived; his grades were great, and his demeanor was always positive. He never seemed to have a bad day or a sad moment. Dahlia kept him busy with after-school activities. He played basketball for the neighborhood boys' team and learned to swim at the YMCA. His room was always neat and tidy in comparison to Simone's, and he did chores without complaint. He loved being in the kitchen with Simone after dinner, preparing their school lunch for the next day.

One night, Dahlia went in to tuck him in for the night, and he read her a short story. She kissed him on the cheek and said, "Good night, little prince. Sleep well. I love you." These words were what she said to her own children when they were younger. Kennedy hugged her and said, "Good night, Mommy. I love you too." Mommy—Simone was the only sibling who had never outgrown calling Dahlia that. She smiled at him as she left the room and turned the light off.

Simone constantly joked in front of Kennedy, "Since you won't let me have a puppy, can we just keep him?" He would giggle and say, "Yeah, can we just keep me?"

Eighteen months after Kennedy was placed with Dahlia, there was still no contact from Amanda Parker. The courts moved to contact every relative connected in any way to Amanda, and there weren't many. No response came back; everyone assumed Amanda was using a different name and didn't want to be located.

Dahlia had filed for adoption after a few months. Now everything moved along expeditiously, and Kennedy's adoption was finalized on his birthday. And what a great day it was. Everyone dressed in their Sunday best. He had picked out a navy-blue suit, a light-blue shirt, a Superman tie, and his dress shoes.

Simone tried to appear nonchalant about the whole affair, but her heart could not have been more excited or proud of her little brother. There were a few close friends, the neighbors next door, and, of course, Liam Wainright and Eden Harper.

Kennedy had begged Dahlia for months to change his last name. He wanted desperately to become a Grant. He even picked out a middle name: Cayden. He thought Kennedy Cayden Grant had a nice ring to it! Cayden was Dahlia's maiden name, and she was honored.

After the formalities, pictures were taken, then they all headed to Gatsby's for a nice dinner hosted by Dahlia. It was Kennedy's favorite dress-up restaurant, and this day was all about celebrating him!

Lacey

I'm either my best friend or my worst enemy.
—Whitney Houston

Lacey was the sweetheart of the group who would give you the shirt off her back without thinking twice. One of those girls in high school—true-to-type stunning looks, homecoming queen, cheerleader, and popular with everyone—Lacey had a big heart and no enemies. She had her flaws (and everyone had some back then), insecurities, a lack of self-esteem, and an obsession with good-looking bad boys. She could pick them. Think of the guys you wanted nothing to do with when you were young, the guys you wouldn't dare bring home to meet your family, and the boys you avoided socially. Those were the ones Lacey pursued with her whole heart. It was as though she had some hidden sign on her forehead that only the bad boys could see.

Lacey married her first loser after her freshman year in college. He was an out-of-work car salesman, divorced, and at least ten years her senior, with an expensive cocaine habit and big dreams. No one ever received a straight answer regarding his age. A smooth talker, Jonathan convinced her she did not need college because she was too beautiful and should pursue a career in modeling.

Lacey worked three different jobs to support the two of them. She worked in an insurance office Monday through Friday from 7:00 a.m. until 2:00 p.m. She tended a bar in a busy exclusive hotel downtown Monday through Thursday from 6:00 p.m. until the place closed. She sold high-end cosmetics at one of the department stores on Friday evenings and all day on Saturdays and Sundays. She loved doing makeovers for wealthy women shopping for a new look every other month.

Thank goodness for tips at the bar and commission checks at the department store, because Jonathan would have her paycheck spent before payroll could get it into their account, not that he was doing anything to help out except talk—talk about businesses he would never start, this management position, or that start-up! He was lazy, he was a sponge, and he controlled Lacey, who really didn't have the backbone to leave him.

That was until Lacey came home very early one day from the insurance office with a bad case of the flu. It was around nine-thirty in the morning, and Jonathan's car was parked out front. She thought, *Oh great, he's sick too!* He said, "I have an interview with another dealership at nine, so I'll be going in to work late." The house was dark, just like she left it. The drapes had not been opened, and the coffee pot was still on. She walked into the bedroom and found her husband entangled in the heap of linen, having sex with another woman in her home, in her bed! How could he?

They didn't see her standing at the foot of the bed. They didn't even see her walk across the room. What broke the moment, the sounds of their moans and groans, was a lamp crashing against the wall. Lacey was beside herself as she screamed at the woman, "Get the hell out of my house!" It was an ultimate betrayal by Jonathan, who had jumped to his feet and was waving his hands as he shouted, "It's not what it looks like! I can explain! Just calm down!"

What Lacey did not know was that since she met Jonathan and married him, this had been a regular occurrence under her own roof. There were just too many women to count. What kind of man does that?

Lacey spent the first night in her adult life alone. She did not sleep and wondered what on earth she would do. She was alone. For many women, this would have been an awakening, a necessary moment of clarity. This was a time to learn, grow, and morph into a more self-reliant, stronger, independent woman.

But that was just not the Lacey everyone knew and loved. She started dating immediately, which led to one bad episode after another. Different wolves were disguised as sheep. A woman who has been treated badly in a relationship usually discovers what she does not want in her next partner, but Lacey was more afraid of being alone and lonely. She needed a man in her life, any man. A cheater with no job, a liar, a thief, or even an abuser was better than no man at all. She had never taken the time to get to know herself or realize just how amazing she was and that she was worthy of real love.

A few months later, they all met Pierce. Lacey had stars in her eyes. Although he cleaned up well and presented himself as charming, intelligent, and educated, it was apparent at social gatherings among the group that at one time or another, Pierce had tried to hit on each of the other women—Chloe, Felicity, Raven, and even Simone. He was very *handsy* with all the women at ATD. Simone was the one to call him out on it. He tried as hard as he could to turn it around, but she wasn't having it! Lacey always simply laughed it off, saying, "Oh, he's just joking around." It was offensive, and it definitely wasn't funny!

Three months later, at Simone and Dietrich's annual barbeque, Lacey shocked everyone by announcing, "We went down to the courthouse. Hey, y'all, we're married!" The four women looked at one another and rolled their eyes with that here-we-go-again look. Unbeknownst to him, the guys did not like Pierce at all. In his self-praising opinion, they were all jealous.

Andre and Drake operated their own software engineering company, Sebastian had his own architectural firm, and Dietrich retired successfully as an entertainment attorney. What on earth was there to be jealous of?

As months passed, Lacey started to seem scattered, absent-minded, and slightly paranoid. It was as though she couldn't make a decision for herself; every movement and every action had to be run by Pierce. She was no longer able to meet her girlfriends once in a while for coffee or brunch on Sunday afternoon. Other than at A Tasty Dish, you never saw Lacey anywhere without Pierce. It was obvious she was being smothered and controlled.

The women had continued their monthly ladies' night out, something they started doing years ago when their daughters were in elementary school, and now the girls were in college. Lacey began to come up with every excuse in the book to bow out. Usually, it was sinus issues, cramps, or "Something I ate didn't agree with me," but everyone knew she did not have a sensitive or discriminating palate. Lacey was very happy with junk food; the greasier, saltier, and sweeter, the better. Raven knew Lacey had always looked forward to these outings. They all knew something was off. They just couldn't figure out what.

Why was their long-time friend isolating herself and pulling away? Lacey was even skipping out on special events to market A Tasty Dish. Anytime the group could make a public appearance and invite people to visit the café, they'd usually all jumped on it. At Chamber of Commerce functions, conferences, festivals, you name it, at least two of them made an appearance. But the ladies could no longer depend on Lacey.

Then it started. Lacey was hiding bruises, scratches, and black eyes. According to Lacey, at this stage of her life, she suddenly turned very clumsy. She was always "falling over this or tripping on that."

Her friends were suspicious, but Lacey would adamantly deny any allegations of physical abuse by Pierce. They just wanted their friend to be happy, and they didn't believe for one minute that Pierce was the answer to that happiness.

Raven

*A best friend is someone who understands your past, believes
in your future, and accepts you for the way you are today.*
                                                  —Bernard Meltzer

Raven and her younger sister, Kayla, were very close even though there was a four-year difference between them. They shared that silent unbreakable bond that many sisters could only wish for. Raven looked after Kayla; and in Kayla's eyes, her sister, Raven, could do no wrong. If Kayla, with her mischievous side, found herself in trouble with their parents—Sidney and Violet—her older sister was quick to defend and sometimes even absorb some of the blame.

By the time the two became adults, Kayla respected Raven as a wife and mother and professionally as a human resources manager, while Raven admired her sister's zest for life and appreciated how hard Kayla studied and worked to reach her own goals.

In high school, Raven had a group of close friends she hung out with. They were popular but not to the point of being cliquish. They were accepted and liked by everyone. They had much of the same interests when it came to music, movies, hobbies, and boys.

In the summer before her senior year in high school, Raven and her friends were invited to a pool party by a senior from a different high school. Raven was a reluctant participant, but her friends were nothing if not persistent. She finally gave in. On a warm Saturday night in July, the five girls piled into one car and drove twenty-two miles to get to this pool party, giggling all the way. Hannah and

Raven had been friends since the fourth grade when Hannah's family moved three doors over.

The reason for attending this party was that Hannah had a major crush on Jensen, the host. His name was actually Matthew Jenson, referred to only by his last name for some reason. Hannah, in her own way, had practically demanded her friends attend this party. Upon arriving, Hannah was the first out of the car, making a beeline through the house to find Jensen, who was in the pool with a few teens, playing a game of volleyball. He gave her a quick nod of acknowledgment and put his focus back on the game. It took Hannah no time to peel off her cover-up and flip-flops and join the competition in the pool.

The girls had split off in different directions. Raven wandered into the den where a tall, good-looking, slender young man was taking on all challengers in Pac-Man. Before the night was over, the quest became evident to other boys that this guy needed to be beaten. As the life of teens went, reputations were at stake. Raven, nursing a can of ginger ale, propped herself against a wall behind the young man, clearly amused at his excitement over his gaming conquests.

Some guy rushed by her, not watching where he was going, almost knocking her off her feet. Soda went flying everywhere. The can made its landing at the champion's feet. As he stood and turned around, he saw Raven standing there, drenched, with a young man making lame apologies. He held out his hand to Raven as he said, "Geez, Kyle. Get lost! You've caused enough trouble already."

The champion escorted Raven to the kitchen, where he pulled towels from a drawer and offered them to her. He smiled as he shook her hand and said, "Hi, my name is Drake. So sorry about that whole fiasco with Kyle. He's a one-man wrecking crew!"

Raven, still trying to mop up spilled soda off her clothes and arms, extended her right hand and said, "Hello, Drake. It's nice to meet you as well. I'm Raven. Accidents happen, but they usually happen to someone else. At least I'll have something to remember this night by."

As the night went on, Drake could not stop smiling, and he never left Raven's side except to fetch another ginger ale. He was not

"Pac driven" anymore. The two of them chatted until the spell was broken by the female voices of Raven's girlfriends, who were tired and ready to call it a night. Drake walked her to the car and asked for her phone number. For Drake and Raven, the night ended way too soon.

Drake was smitten. He had a grin on his face all day on Sunday around the house with his parents and two brothers. The teasing from his brothers, Davis and Aiden, was relentless. He found himself unable to focus on the task of helping get Aiden's new car stereo installed. He wanted desperately to call Raven just to hear her voice, which he thought was the sweetest sound he had ever heard. Listening to her and reminiscing about their conversation the previous night made him well aware that Raven was not like any girl he had ever met. She was very smart and had a ladylike quality beyond her years. He realized they talked about what seemed like everything. Plus, they had so much in common.

Drake finally gave in and called Raven that evening after dinner. Twenty minutes into the conversation, he asked if she'd be interested in going to the Duffy Street arcade on Saturday. Duffy's was a fun and popular place for older teens to meet and socialize.

To be admitted into the arcade, you had to be sixteen years old with ID. Plus, you'd have to pay a $5 cover charge. Business hours during the summer months were Sunday, Tuesday, Wednesday, and Thursday from 3:00 p.m. to 10:00 p.m. On Friday and Saturday nights, Duffy's was open until 11:30 p.m. and closed every Monday.

Duffy's had everything from music to pinball machines to air hockey to digital Trivial Pursuit to Pac-Man to ping-pong and from pool tables to popcorn to root beer floats to pizza by the slice to most stuff in between preferred by teens, and they had dancing in the basement. There was always adult supervision at Duffy's, not that the kids ever got in trouble, just an occasional disagreement over high school sports rivalries during the school year, which was never serious enough for the adults to intervene, and there was absolutely no loitering at any time in the parking lot.

Raven and Drake spoke on the telephone every day after that initial Sunday evening phone call.

The next week at the Duffy Street arcade was the first date for the couple, but unlike most first dates, this was different. There were no awkward moments of silence. Drake did everything right: he opened doors, including car doors, and pulled out chairs. The two were very comfortable with each other. They both knew other people in attendance at Duffy's that evening, and when approached, Raven or Drake would introduce the other accordingly with a beaming expression.

Drake was impressed with her competitive side; it was an unexpected surprise. He had always been a play-to-win kind of guy with his buddies. But in a few rounds of air hockey, Raven beat him every time, delivering a taste of defeat, which he took it quite well as she laughed and said, "If you can't play with the big dogs, stay on the porch!" He gave her a friendly hug. He felt that she could beat him at anything, and he would just keep smiling as long as he could be around her. Raven challenged Drake, which was one of the many things he really liked about her.

The two dated throughout their senior year even though they attended different high schools. Drake and Raven supported each other in every aspect of their lives; they were a team. She cheered him on at many of his basketball games and track meets, just as he was there in the back of the auditorium for most, if not all, of her debates. In the last year, she was one of five students from the city to compete all the way up to state level. Raven won first place in the current-events debate "The Growing Power of Women in Politics."

Drake and Raven went on to attend two different universities within the state system. The distance was not bad, and they were both so busy at school that time seemed to fly by. Holidays, summer, and other breaks were magical for the couple. The two families spent time together whenever the couple was home, and they blended well together.

A few years after college graduation, Drake knew Raven was the love of his life. He wanted to face the world with her, have children with her, grow old with her, and spend the rest of his life with her. It made perfect sense to him, and he was pretty certain she felt the same way. They had whispered those three little words to each other.

On Christmas Day, Drake insisted on dropping off Raven's gift early in the morning. He knew Sidney, Violet, and Kayla would be at church, so he was able to get some alone time with her before the chaos of the holiday with the family began. He was nervous, his mouth was dry, and his palms were sweaty after he removed his gloves.

He asked Raven for a glass of water, and when she left the room, he put the neatly wrapped box he had been carrying in his arms under the beautifully decorated tree with all the other gifts. Raven took notice, assuming it was a sweater or jacket, always something practical she could use, and Drake had very good taste in the gifts he bought for her. Raven thought when she returned to the room that maybe he was coming down with some kind of flu.

Drake had seated himself on the sofa, taking the water with one hand and pulling Raven to sit next to him with the other. He took a big gulp of water and then began to speak slowly and deliberately. He kissed her on the forehead. He was lost in her eyes. "You know how much I love you, and I know you love me just as much. I begin and end all my days thinking of you, then I find myself staring off into space, daydreaming. All day long, I wonder how you're doing and what you're doing, and I ask myself, 'Is she thinking of me as well?' I know we're happy when we're together, but I want that all the time. I want you to be the mother of my children. I want to grow old with you. Make me the happiest man on earth right here right now. Tell me you'll marry me!"

By this time, Drake was on one knee, holding her left hand in his left hand as he pulled a beautiful marquise-cut diamond ring out of his pocket with his right hand. It sparkled brilliantly under the low lights of the room. Raven's jaw dropped. She smiled, hugged Drake, and cried at the same time, whispering in his ear, "Yes! Yes! Of course, I'll marry you, and we can be two of the happiest people on earth!" Drake found her smile radiant, lighting up the room. Their joy filled the room as they both cried and laughed together. Neither one of them could wait to share the news with family and friends. It was a Christmas they would remember for the rest of their lives.

After a long engagement, in early fall almost two years later, Drake and Raven married in a traditional Catholic ceremony. It was a beautiful day. It was sunny, the autumn colors had turned, the air was crisp and clean, and the temperature outside was perfect.

Sidney and Violet were so happy to see their firstborn so in love and married, as well as Nathaniel and Sophie, their eldest son having taken those vows of holy matrimony not too long after. Kayla, as the maid of honor, stepped up to her role incredibly well with the help of Raven's girlfriends. She was so pretty and possessed a sophisticated innocence. Drake's brothers, as attendants, were all handsome and dapper that day. The ceremony was beautiful, and the reception turned out to be a gala event. It was one of the happiest and most wonderful occasions for both families.

The newlyweds had a beautiful start to their lives together. Drake and Raven focused on their careers while planning for the future. Drake was in high demand as a go-to IT guru at his company, but he constantly wondered what it would be like to run his own company. The two of them knew they had secure jobs with stable companies. When the time came to start a family, their future couldn't have been brighter.

Two years later, the welcomed a baby girl! Reese Alexis St. Claire arrived in this world two weeks early. She was very small at two pounds and six ounces. Reese's heart and lungs were weak, and the doctors decided to keep her in the hospital until they could get her up to at least five pounds. Plus, as a precaution, they would be able to keep a close watch on her heart and lungs.

The time came for Raven to be discharged. She was leaving the hospital without her baby. The new mom had already joked with the nurses about taking care of Reese until she could return after getting settled at home. An exhausted and devastated Raven did not sleep that first night. She counted the hours until she could drive back to the hospital and hold her baby in her arms.

Raven arrived just before the babies started to wake in time for feeding, still tired but overjoyed to be in the NICU, holding Reese. After two weeks, Raven and Drake listened carefully as the doctor told them he was discharging Reese as she had gained weight and was very strong.

Things went from zero to sixty, and years flew by as Reese grew into an incredible young woman. She was a National Honor Society member and a talented musician who was very intelligent, practical, and beautiful. She was comfortable with her career choice, and her colleagues respected her professionalism and drive.

Simone

*I have a feeling that I make a very good friend, I am a good
mother, a good sister, and a good citizen. I am involved in life
itself—all of it. I have a lot of energy and a lot of nerve.*

—Maya Angelou

Simone was the eldest of the group only by a few years. She
looked great for her age, and if you asked her, "What's your
secret to fighting wrinkles?" she'd laugh and say, "Estee Lauder
or Lancôme, take your pick, and sometimes a bit of biting, kicking,
scratching, and screaming helps!"

Always protective as well as very loyal to her family and friends,
she possessed a profound maternal instinct. Simone was fiercely
independent and focused on her career. After college, she dated, but
there was no serious relationship in the cards for her. Usually, after
the second date, if she wasn't feeling some kind of potential, she'd
think, *Why waste the time?*

Simone wanted butterflies and fireworks! Men found her attractive, although to some, her confidence was a big turnoff. She had
plenty of male friends, and as always, even in high school, with her
outgoing personality and understanding of all things sports, she very
easily became every guy's *buddy.*

During the holidays, when Simone was thirty-eight, she was
busy as usual with her life in San Diego. She was preparing for the
drive to Los Angeles for the great Christmas gathering of Dahlia's
side of the family. There would be plenty of cousins, aunts, uncles,
grandparents, and a host of very close friends passing through Aunt

Candice's for most of the day. Dahlia's sister held an open house from ten in the morning on Christmas Day until two that afternoon. People making their way through town between destinations could stop in and get their fill of finger foods, appetizers, hot apple cider with whipped cream and cinnamon, coffee, tea, or hot chocolate.

The formal family dinner started at three sharp, and Candice was a stickler for being prompt. Simone, Dahlia, and younger sister Faith had this tradition down to a fine art. Each of them had special talents, so each year, Christmas Day was pretty much routine for them, from decorating and prep work to food for the guests passing through to the dinner to beverages and even desserts to scheduling carols to opening presents. They loved fussing over their family, but they were exhausted and happy when the day was over.

As Simone drove north, she thought about what she would say when the subject of marriage and her prospects for such came up. It was always one of the favorite subjects of the older women during any big event. Simone decided that this year, she'd share her true feelings on the matter. "I will probably never get married, and that's fine. I am truly happy with who I am. I get plenty of male attention, I have a successful career, I make good money, and I work hard so I can play hard. C'mon, you all know I take great vacations! So you can simply stop asking. After all, a husband isn't everything."

She hoped that after making such a statement, they would give the subject a rest, at least until Easter.

A week later, just before New Year's Eve, Simone received a phone call from a dating service she had won a free membership to from a raffle. She had been so busy at the time that after a few dates, she asked them to put her on the *back burner*. An assistant had signed up a new member, a prominent attorney who had just relocated from New York to San Diego just before Christmas.

From his profile, Dietrich Essex was a perfect match for Simone Grant. At least Lucia, the assistant, thought so; therefore, she contacted Simone immediately to inquire if she was still single and interested in meeting Dietrich. Simone was surprised. From Lucia's description, this guy sounded decent, and what did she have to lose? Even after reminding Lucia that the last couple of guys they introduced her to turned out to be "less than three on a scale of one to ten!"

Simone relented and gave Lucia the green light to give Dietrich her phone number. That first call lasted for a couple of hours. After the first and second dates, it was pretty much smooth sailing. Simone and Dietrich were both all in, and by May, they were already planning on combining households. They both knew this was the *one*!

Dietrich proposed to Simone on her fortieth birthday. He took her to Las Vegas and did all the planning…and the rest was history! They married in Vegas eight months later, with plenty of family and friends present for the ceremony at an elegant little chapel on the strip.

Three years after that, they met an eighteen-month-old foster child named Tula in May. Dietrich was immediately scheduled to travel to Chicago, New York, and Singapore to meet with his exclusive clients. After a few months of visits by Simone and Dietrich when he was available, Tula was placed into the Essex home. Dietrich made arrangements to get home for their first Christmas together. It was a surprise for Tula, who would inevitably become a daddy's girl. Her face would light up whenever he called home, and she'd have the biggest smile ever from just hearing his voice.

Tula was formally adopted by the Essex after Dietrich's travels ended. Her name was changed to Tallulah Honor Essex. The little girl beamed with joy as she thanked the judge for "my new mommy and daddy!"

As the years progressed, Tallulah did very well in school. She was rewarded for her grades and efforts with dinners out in which she got to pick out the restaurant or an impromptu trip to the mall. Tallulah was competitive in everything she did; she wanted to be the best. Dreams and goals were always encouraged by Simone and Dietrich, along with humility. Be a gracious winner and even more so when you lose.

When Tallulah started high school, Simone had been suffering from migraines. They were bad, and by the end of each day, she was exhausted. Finally, one morning, Simone had trouble getting dressed. She was holding on to the walls to balance. Plus, she could hardly speak. Dietrich joked "Honey, you know you sound completely ine-briated." Thirty minutes had gone by, and Simone still had trouble getting dressed.

Once Tallulah left for school, Dietrich let his wife know he was calling 911 for an ambulance.

Simone begged him not to, saying that she just needed coffee! He helped her get dressed. He was taking her to the ER to find out what was going on. Simone had her flip-flops on, and when they arrived at the hospital, her Nikes were still in her hand when Dietrich came out with a wheelchair.

In the ER, Simone was seen right away. Tests were done, and scans were ordered. They needed to find out what this was! Simone and Dietrich anxiously waited and waited some more. About two-thirty in the afternoon, two doctors walked into the room to advise the couple, "Simone has suffered a stroke. It's a good thing you brought her in when you did. The next twenty-four hours are going to be critical. She could have another stroke. We also discovered a large tumor in the frontal lobe of her brain."

The two of them sat in silence after the doctors left the room. They called Dietrich's parents—Lars and Ava—immediately and asked them to pick up Tallulah from school. They sent their grand-daughter a text: "We will pick you up at 3:45 from the Dairy Queen around the corner from your school." This would alleviate the head-ache of traffic around campus and the massive high school traffic at McDonald's after school.

Tallulah was standing outside with a fresh bottle of water when her grandparents drove into the parking lot. She got in the car, greeting them, but she knew something was off and inquired. They explained as best they could: "Dear, your mom has been admitted to the hospital. She's fine but they want to take precautions." The teen-ager decided not to press with more questions; she knew her father would tell her everything once she saw him. The ride was long and silent.

They validated their parking and got directions at the courtesy desk. Tallulah tried to walk slower to allow her grandparents to keep up. But patience was not a strong trait with her, and everyone knew it, especially in times like this.

When they exited the elevator, they saw Dietrich standing in the hallway, speaking with a nurse. Tallulah rushed to reach him but stopped short of interrupting. She looked up and saw the open door where her mother was lying. She entered walking over to the bed. "Well, Mother dear, what kind of trouble have you gotten yourself into now?" She thought of how her mother, someone with an overwhelming presence, looked small.

Simone smiled at her daughter and said, "You know me. I wanted some time off, and this would guarantee me some downtime."

At that moment, Dietrich walked in with an entourage behind him, Lars, Ava, a nurse, and two doctors. The doctors approached the bedside and asked, "Simone, do you know why you're here?"

Silence filled the room, then Simone responded, "They have told me I had a stroke."

Heads nodded in agreement. "Anything else?"

Simone continued, "Yes, they also told me you found a brain tumor."

Heads nodded again. You could tell just by being in the room that they felt sorry for the patient.

Tallulah's eyes began to tear a little, but Simone wasn't done. "You guys have missed the big picture. You found a brain!"

Laughter erupted in the room. The doctors looked baffled. It was a typical Simone style; she had jokes.

Tallulah whispered in her father's ear, "Oh snap! Dad, I realize Mom's going to be just fine! Who gets devastating news and has a witty comeback like that? Only Simone Essex!"

Simone hadn't eaten anything in over twenty-four hours. She was starving. Dietrich and Tallulah took turns giving her ice chips. After that, Simone was settled in for the night, and they all said their goodbyes. Dietrich left specific instructions at the nurse's station to contact him with any changes during the night regardless of the time. He gave them his cell number, his home number, and his parents' numbers as well.

Simone slept peacefully through the night. At home, Dietrich insisted Tallulah go to school. He promised his daughter, who was almost in tears, that she could go to the hospital after school. He left for the hospital early, hoping to get there before Simone woke up.

Dietrich was beside himself when he was greeted by the nurse at the desk in the neuro ICU with "Good morning. Your wife is awake. She had another stroke around one o'clock this morning!"

Dietrich, a man who never shouted except at a sporting event, lost his cool. He kept playing over and over what the doctor said: "The next twenty-four hours are critical. She could have another stroke." Simone was unaware but could hear her husband's voice, and he didn't sound happy at all.

When Lars and Ava arrived, their son updated them. He was livid. No one knew what conversations took place with whom. By one-thirty that afternoon, Simone was being ambulanced over to a different hospital. He sent Tallulah a text explaining that Simone was being moved to a different hospital, still in neuro ICU. He would arrange a ride for her.

Tallulah texted him back, "Dad, don't worry about me. I'll get a ride. Just take care of my mommy."

Simone didn't have a clue as to why Dietrich was having her moved to another hospital. The ambulance ride took less than twenty minutes without sirens. New doctors, new nurses, a new location—this could be dreadful for some, but Simone was best at playing with whatever hand she was dealt. She loved a quote she saw in college that said, "Life is 10 percent what happens to you and 90 percent what you do with what happens to you!"

Simone was wheeled into her new room by the paramedics. She thanked them "for the wild ride." Within a few minutes, Dietrich arrived, followed by his parents. The nurse introduced herself as Isabelle. She was pretty and polite and spoke with a very British accent. The doctors were friendly, seeming a bit more assertive than those at the previous hospital.

Simone found out the hard way that she was completely paralyzed, even unable to hold a pen and sign documents. Dietrich signed for her as her power of attorney. When Tallulah witnessed this, it was difficult to see her mother so physically weak and frail. These two words were never ever used to describe Simone.

She was in very bad shape, but after a few hours, her sense of humor was evident to the entire staff in the neuro ICU. Simone knew it was going to take some time; patience; and her own positive, kick-ass attitude to get her to the other side of this. She was still able to manage a smile.

Tallulah pulled a Walgreens shopping bag from her backpack. First, she took out a small bag of new hair ties and headbands. She gently pulled her mother's braided hair into a ponytail, adding one of the headbands, telling Simone, "Now, Miss Matchy-Matchy, you're all color coordinated! Drab gray with accessories too." It made them all feel good to see Simone smile and hear her laugh.

Simone would need a miracle. She would die or be in a wheelchair for the rest of her life. At best, she would need therapy, physical, occupational, and speech. That was if she could even get around on her own. Plus, she would need to get stronger before brain surgery. The tumor had to be removed.

Since Simone was going to be away from home for weeks, Dietrich and Tallulah put together a few items for her room. One was a split picture frame with a picture of the family on one side, and the other side had a photo of Simone and Stabler (the dog). Yes, he was named after one of Simone's favorite characters on *Law & Order*.

Father and daughter stayed up late one Friday night to create a playlist of her of all her favorite music. That was a challenge because Simone's taste covered almost everything from Pachelbel to Vivaldi to David Sanborn to Train to anything '60s or '70s. He found an updated version by Dave Koz of the song he played when he first told her he loved her: "This Guy's in Love with You." He knew that just hearing it would make her smile.

After two hundred days in the hospital, two strokes, an intensive brain surgery, and some excruciating therapy, Simone pulled through like a champion. She was back on her feet, spending a week with a walker and a week with a cane, and after that, Simone demanded to walk on her own. She had trouble figuring out what to do first. Dietrich went to play golf one day while Tallulah was at school, and he returned to find his wife standing on the formal dining room table, cleaning the chandelier. He was speechless. After all, what could he say? Simone was going to do whatever she wanted to do! She wanted to have a small dinner party to try her new recipe for lobster ravioli. She kept herself very busy.

Simone eventually saw a small bistro for sale in the paper one day. She didn't say anything but made a point to drive by as soon as she could. Once she saw the place, her brain would not shut down, so she finally approached Dietrich. She could use some of her inheritance from her own father and his parents.

Dietrich was proud that Simone had done all her homework first. He drew up all the legal paperwork, and Simone made an offer. Then she would sell the idea to her friends! That was how A Tasty Dish started.

Lines Crossed

*Sometimes we need to be destroyed by a situation
before we understand how bad it was for us.*
—Karen Waddell

Whenever the other four women tried to fix Lacey up with decent men, she did everything in her power to sabotage the budding relationship early on. Is there really such a thing as a guy being "too nice"? In a novel from 1992 called *Waiting to Exhale* by Terry McMillan, during conversation at a birthday celebration between female friends, one character stated, "It's hard to go back to bullshit when you've been treated like a queen!" Four of this group of five women opted for being treated like a queen.

By the time Chloe, Felicity, Raven, and Simone figured out that their suspicions were true, things were pretty far out of control, and Lacey was ten feet deep in denial. All they could do was discreetly let her know that they were there for her and that she needed help desperately. Lacey would have to take the first step for herself. Pierce's inappropriate behavior had escalated, becoming too reckless, brash, and shameful. Everyone had their guards up, and he was constantly making unwanted advances and giving uninvited attention, even including touching other staff and patrons. It was almost as though he didn't care. The worst part was that he had convinced Lacey that his wandering eyes and hands were all her own fault.

At the A Tasty Dish Christmas party, Simone hired a professional photographer, who made the rounds, taking candid shots of different groups, couples, and kids. She wanted him to capture various fun moments of the evening. While taking a group photo of the entire staff and their significant others, Pierce situated himself between Lacey and Felicity. He put his arms around their waists. When the photographer told everyone to smile, he grabbed Felicity's butt. Simone was livid as she caught the action out of the corner of her eye, and Pierce realized he was busted by the one person he did not like at all. He felt as though Simone tolerated him. It did not help whenever someone said, "Oh, she's a great judge of character." Maybe he felt that she could see through him and knew what kind of twisted heart he possessed, if he had a heart at all.

After dinner and desserts, gifts were raffled off to the staff, and all the kids received goody bags and a little dance-floor time. The night was winding down. People started saying their goodbyes and packing their cars to leave the venue. Simone was leaning into the cargo area of her SUV, arranging packages and waiting for Dietrich. Someone walked up and pressed himself against her from behind, then reached around, grabbing her breast. She chuckled, "Oh, aren't you feeling your Wheaties tonight!" It was her husband being playful, Simone thought, then she slowly turned to kiss him and gasped! It was Pierce, and he was obviously feeling pretty good after drinking for most of the evening. "Simone, you always smell so good. I bet you smell good all over, if you know what I mean. What's that perfume you're wearing?" She was completely repulsed by his touch.

Simone quickly smacked his hands away; and in her best "you don't want to mess with me" voice, the one she used only in situations like this, she sternly and adamantly said, "Pierce, one of these days, you're going to put your hands on the wrong woman, and there's going to be hell to pay. Now get your drunken ass away from me and don't ever put your filthy hands on me again!"

Pierce grumbled under his breath, "Bitch," as he staggered away. Simone was so angry that she was shaking when she settled herself in the passenger seat and watched as Dietrich approached the vehicle, having no idea of what just took place. She saw him wave goodbye to Pierce. When they arrived home, Simone was tired and angry and decided not to tell him about Pierce until the next day, after a good night's sleep. She had been in a good mood and would still be upset in the morning, but she was not going to let the parasite ruin this night for her.

By Valentine's Day, things were worse than ever. Pierce possessed a vicious side no one had ever seen. They knew he could be mean and verbally cruel. He was being his usual obnoxious self, and Lacey was jumpier than ever. A week later, Lacey called Simone on her mobile "I need you to pick me up at my place now. Pierce won't let me leave! I need a safe place to stay for a couple of nights!" She could tell by Lacey's voice that her friend was in a horrible situation. "Just how bad is it?" was the million-dollar question.

It was six in the evening, and Simone was at the gym, getting ready for a swim in the warm-water pool. Simone went back to the locker room, got dressed, signed out, and texted Dietrich, "Going to p/u Lacey. Not sure what's going on. P won't let her leave. Be home soon. Love, Si!"

Dietrich got the message and responded with a text begging her not to go to Lacey's alone but to drive by and pick him up. Simone was already in the car and ignored the incoming text. In desperation, Dietrich tried calling his wife, but as usual, Simone was a woman on a mission. When she got to Lacey's house, she parked her car in front of the house on the street, turned off the engine, saw Pierce's car and Lacey's car, let out a sigh while walking to the door, and placed her key fob in her bra. She smiled to herself and thought, *Geez, it's only Pierce. It's not like I need my pepper spray!*

Simone rang the doorbell, and Pierce opened the door with a hideous grin on his face. Simone called out, "Lacey, I'm here! It's time to go!" She glanced across the room for her friend and saw that the place was in shambles, furniture overturned and table lamps on the floor. The place had never looked like this before. The door slammed close, startling her. Simone turned around to find Pierce standing there within striking distance. His shirt was opened, with a loose tie hanging around his neck. His long sleeves were rolled up to the elbow. There was blood on the collar, and she saw his belt lying on the floor. His hair was disheveled. He was a hot and sweaty mess!

Simone knew she needed to run, but fear had gripped her and left her frozen in place. Then she saw the switchblade in his right hand. Before she could react, he lunged at her, grabbing her by the throat with his left hand. In a flash, Pierce had her pinned against the wall. As he held her, she could smell the bourbon in his breath. Simone thought about Lacey. Was she already dead or clinging to life in another room? The room felt cold and tight. Simone felt terror overtake her body, making it impossible to think clearly. She tried to maintain her focus while feeling pain around her neck. She thought that she could possibly be taking her last breaths. She wasn't physically able to defend herself.

Pierce growled like some kind of wild animal, his breath just inches away from her face, and with every horrible word he spoke, his vile spit was hitting her face. "I could do anything I want to you right now, and nobody would care. I think that man of yours would thank me! I could choke the life out of you with my bare hands or slit your throat from ear to ear. What's it gonna be, you self-righteous bitch?"

Just then, Lacey emerged from the bedroom, limping slowly, with both arms crossed over her stomach, a weekend bag over her shoulder, and sunglasses on long after the sun had set. She screamed at what she was witnessing. "Pierce, this is between you and me. Please don't drag anyone else into our business!" At that moment Simone who had been frightened to her core realized her friend was alive. Pierce relaxed his grip on her neck, she was able to kick him in the groin, and he was neutralized for the moment. Enough time for the two women to escape, as they got into Simone's car, they could see Pierce stumbling out the front door. Simone pressed the ignition, and the tires screeched in one fluid motion. Neither woman ever looked back.

When Simone pulled into the garage at her home, where a frantic Dietrich was waiting, he had been beside himself, and getting no response from his wife on her mobile didn't help. She took her friend's jacket and hung it on the coat rack.

Everything happened so fast that she had never really looked at Lacey's face, but in the light of their kitchen, she could see that her lip was bleeding, that her nose was bloody, and that her cheek was swollen. Both eyes were black, the left swollen shut, and she had a

nasty scrape on her right temple. Her shirt was torn. There was bruising around her neck plus scratches, scrapes, and cuts on her arms and
shoulders. Lacey was truly defeated, physically and mentally broken.
She couldn't tell them her husband had also savagely and brutally
raped her. All Simone knew was that one day, things would escalate
and that Pierce was surely well on his way to killing his wife. This
could have been that day!

If he was crazy enough to do what he had just done…then he
was definitely a danger to everyone. Simone was talking fast as she
rattled off the events that had unfolded. The only thing Dietrich
heard clearly was "And he slammed the door behind me. He was on
me as soon as I turned around. He choked me and pulled a switchblade on me!" He took a hard look at Lacey and glanced back at
Simone. His eyes grew wide, and his voice got loud. "Whoa, back
up! He did what? Oh, hell no! Somebody needs to give that asshole a
beatdown like he's been beating on Lacey, and I'm just the guy to do
it! Nobody treats women like that, and nobody, I mean nobody, lays
a hand on my wife!"

Dietrich spun around to grab his car keys, but Simone was on
her feet and got to the counter first. She said as she grabbed the keys,
"What you're going to do right now, love, is calm down. We've called
the police. We'll let them handle Pierce, and right about now, he
has got pain in his groin!" Her husband was concerned by Lacey's
condition as well as the bruises on his own wife's neck. She smiled
and worked overtime to lighten the mood, which was what Simone
always managed to do; it was her gift of timing.

Frightened yet angry, the two women felt better while waiting
for the police to arrive, and Dietrich served up the salmon salad he
had made for dinner. Simone felt safe at home. From Californian
days past, they'd always kept their home secure. It was their sanc-
tuary. Lacey knew she was safe. The couple thought about letting
her stay in the cottage by the pool but decided to keep her closer,
specifically in the guestroom downstairs. She would have her own
bathroom and plenty of privacy. Simone told Lacey that she could
stay as long as she needed.

This was the last straw; hopefully, Lacey was finally done with Pierce. Two uniformed officers arrived and introduced themselves as Natasha De Luca and Isaac Fontaine. After a few seconds, Simone and Dietrich could tell that this was not the first time Lacey and the officers had been face-to-face. The officers were standing there, stoic and compassionate, while Lacey was fighting back the urge to show the tears welling up in her eyes. Natasha spoke softly as she pulled out her notepad, "Mrs. Williams, tell me you are ready to end this cycle."

Lacey suddenly burst into tears; it was a release of raw emotion. Simone was able to comfort and reassure her friend as she told the officers every sordid detail of her ordeal earlier that evening at the hands of a man who claimed he loved Lacey. When Lacey described her ordeal, she realized that she had endured six long hours as Pierce had held her captive and tortured her. After taking their statements, Natasha, the senior officer, advised them that they would bring them to the emergency room to have a rape kit done on Lacey and have pictures taken of both of their injuries.

Isaac Fontaine spoke, saying, "We have enough to arrest Pierce Williams on several domestic charges including first-degree battery, first-degree rape, and false imprisonment, for starters. I'm sure we can find some more violations."

At the hospital, the officers explained the seventy-two-hour provision of a TRO (temporary restraining order), in which Pierce could have no contact with either of the women, and that would allow Lacey time to petition the court for a permanent restraining order.

Natasha De Luca completed the necessary paperwork for their report, provided them with a case number of the incident, and put an arm around Lacey's shoulder. Dietrich walked the officers to the elevator, and Natasha told him, "Those two women are both very lucky. She's lucky your wife arrived when she did. I hope she realizes this is a serious wake-up call. Some women don't get that!"

Officers at the precinct knew Lacey and Pierce by first name. They had offered her resources before, but she never followed through. She had never even pressed charges against her abusive husband because Pierce always swore it would never happen again—until it did. And it always happened again.

Pierce was taken into custody without incident five minutes after four in the morning. He was unable to post bail immediately, so he was able to sleep off his drunken stupor in jail. Just after two o'clock in the morning, the trio was back at the Essex home, and Lacey was settled in for the night in the guest room. She tried to sleep. She had sent text messages to Chloe, Felicity, and Raven with instructions to steer clear of Pierce, saying she would be at Simone's for a few days until she could get things in order, which included filing a restraining order against him and getting him out of her home and her life.

From the very beginning, when they first met Pierce, they noticed that he dropped by the café daily and always made some kind of scene, from complaining about the food or the service, not that he ever paid for so much as a cup of coffee, to even fussing about whether the temperature in the café was too hot or cold, and he always reminded the waitstaff to be nice to him "because I'm really tight with the owners, and one word from me could get you fired."

Have any interaction with him for more than five minutes, and you'd know Pierce was not a good person. The daily patrons regarded him as a user, a person with no conscience who would take advantage of his own mother if it would benefit him in any way. By most opinions, Pierce was self-serving and just plain evil, but Lacey loved him. Everyone knew she could do better.

Maybe an order of no contact was just what Lacey needed. Pierce would not be able to intimidate her into backing down. During this time, Lacey insisted that she would still be able to handle her responsibilities at A Tasty Dish as usual. Also, she did not want them walking on eggshells when she was around. It was to be business as usual. Her friends let her know that if she needed any time off for any reason, they'd have her back and cover for her. Simone insisted they could all pitch in to cover for Lacey until the swelling and bruising weren't so apparent. At least the visible scars would heal.

When Pierce was served his copy of the TRO (temporary restraining order), he realized he had gone too far. He had pressed his luck in the continued attempt to control and abuse Lacey. That was why the P-RO was granted days after Lacey called the police on the way to Simone's.

Pierce had to move out of Lacey's home. Thank goodness she never added him to the mortgage, not that he ever paid a bill or paid for anything. As a matter of fact, Pierce moved in with the clothes on his back, a car full of clothing and toiletries, and an attitude that said he had hit pay dirt with Lacey. He was a sponge, a leech. He had lost his meal ticket. He could not call or come into ATD, and he had to steer clear of Lacey and Simone.

In the past, there had been police calls to the Williams residence by neighbors. Pierce would be arrested, and before the ink was dry, Lacey was there to bail him out. Plus, she would never bother to press charges. But this was the real wake-up call for her. Now there were pictures, a police report, and an RO, and Pierce had hurt someone else. He was out of control, and Simone had a firsthand account of exactly what he was capable of.

Once the restraining order went into effect, everyone at ATD was able to breathe a little easier, and the atmosphere became relaxed again; no one constantly looked over their shoulders or had the feeling of dread if Pierce walked in. The café was fun and festive again. Even the regular customers were able to enjoy their meals without the fear of him throwing the place into chaos.

Murder First

One of the scariest things in the world is that other
people can make life-changing decisions for you.
                                    —Karishma Magvani

It was early morning, before sunlight rose over the east to reveal a brand-new day and the waking sounds of a busy city. The shadows of night creatures were starting to disappear as Simone and Walker stepped into the café through the front door, the overnight air heavy and still. The opening and closing team always parked on the street by the front entrance, beneath the illumination of the street lights, instead of across the street, in the lot reserved for employees. Simone had a handicap plate on her car, and as soon as other staff members arrived for their shifts, she would move her car to the lot as well.

Simone and Walker did their morning walk-through and found everything as it should be. They went about their various routines, getting ready for the day ahead. Walker was expecting his weekly delivery. He attempted to open the back door, which led to the delivery and service entrance, but it was stuck. Something on the outside was impeding the exit. He thought of going through the front and taking a walk around back since the sun was beginning to show itself. Walker knew he was strong enough to push the door open, but it was just too hard, so he called for Simone. Maybe the two of them could push the door and remove the obstruction.

They both pushed with all their might, and the door gave way. Walker could see that the garbage dumpster had been moved directly against the door. He said to Simone, "Wow, I wonder how that got that there?"

She responded, "I'll have to see who closed last night. It should have been Lacey or Felicity."

Walker pushed the dumpster so he could open the door all the way, and once he was outside, he almost tripped over something at his feet. He spun around and looked down; and Simone, now in the kitchen, could hear him shout, *"Oh my God! What the hell?"* She quickly ran to the back entrance of the café. The only thing that slowed her down was the vision she caught below the dumpster.

There was a casually dressed male lying facedown on the pavement. One of his legs seemed to be trapped by the wheel of the large refuse bin. Simone let out a loud gasp and put her hands over her mouth. Simone used her foot to gently kick the man, thinking he could be drunk or high. By the looks of his attire, he definitely didn't seem homeless, but he didn't move. Curious as they both were, Walker pulled out his cell phone and dialed 911. Who was this man? Why was he behind A Tasty Dish? Not realizing her lip was bleeding from biting it, Simone looked up from the still body, glanced over at Walker, and shook her head. Her heart was pounding so hard that she thought she could feel each beat.

Walker and Simone waited for the police inside the café. The place was locked and secure.

The police station was less than 2,500 feet from the café. A squad car and an undercover unit arrived out front in what felt like instantly. A detective in plain clothes introduced himself as Mason Asher, possessing a handsome boyish face. He looked all of thirty, but if you looked close enough, you could see the long hours he had put into solving his homicide cases. He had visited the café on several occasions for breakfast, coffee, and sweets on the go plus maybe lunch once or twice. He had a sweet tooth with a weakness for their variety of desserts.

Mason was a cynic, the type of cop who always knew he had the right suspect instantly. To him, it was just a matter of putting the puzzle pieces together and a feeling deep within his gut. It was always the person who denied knowing anything about the crime, the criminal who thought they were the smartest person in the room and so much smarter than the cops.

The uniformed officer, Sonya Teague, standing at five feet seven, had been on the force for four years. She was an attractive bleached blonde who underneath two coats of makeup, apparently loved her tanning-bed time. Teague had a somewhat terse attitude. She had plenty to learn from her superior about tact, fairness, and compassion. Sonya always drew her conclusions early in a case and wouldn't bend on her opinions. Fortunately for her, Mason knew she was a good cop who desperately wanted to be a detective. He was a great mentor and a top lead investigator, so he was willing to overlook her idiosyncrasies most of the time.

Asher and Teague were escorted through the café to the back entrance by Simone, and Walker trailed behind. The detective called for a CSU as he stood over the body of his victim. He was quick to give logistics and other instructions. He asked if the body had been moved. Walker offered an explanation for the dumpster blocking the door and said that they hadn't moved the body. Teague was instructed to go inside and immediately separate the two witnesses.

All four looked up, and the mobile crime scene unit blocked the service driveway. The first thing they did was block the entrance to the service area, securing it with crime scene tape, moving like soldiers who knew their tasks. Each went about it accordingly. Simone and Walker went back inside with officer Teague, and Asher assured her that he would be inside to help her to get statements shortly. Like a military drill sergeant, he was seemingly barking orders at the CSU team. He wanted answers as soon as he could get them, and for Mason Asher, that meant yesterday.

Sitting silently at two different tables by the kitchen, ten feet apart from each other, Walker and Simone stared at each other silently while Officer Teague paced back and forth between them, almost looking down her nose at them. They both exhaled a sigh of relief as the detective entered the kitchen to take over the information gathering. He told the officer to question Walker in the kitchen and that he would speak with Simone.

Asher wasn't interested in intimidating anyone, unlike Teague. He just wanted the facts, the truth with any knowledge of who this victim was and why he was at the service entrance of the café. Mason wanted Simone to feel comfortable. She offered up coffee for the four of them before the serious business of interrogation started. Simone desperately needed the coffee. Her hands were shaking as she brought the cups and an insulated carafe with muffins on a tray. When she finally sat down, she took several deep breaths to slow her breathing. Her heart was still racing. Now that she had a warm cup to hold on to, she hoped calm would set in soon. She had never seen a dead body in such a state.

Simone had never witnessed anything like this before. She was nervous. Asher began with the typical line of questioning. He asked, "Who closed the shop last night? Have you or any of your staff been having problems with anyone?" Before she could answer, Asher's cell phone rang, Simone was grateful for the interruption. The CSU team had rolled the body over. There was no wallet and no identification, and the hands were fingerprinted and bagged. Plus, he had a vial of cocaine in his pocket. The CSU team took a picture of the victim's face and sent it to the detective. Their victim had taken two bullets in the chest. Someone wanted this guy gone.

As usual, Lacey closed the place down the night before and did a thorough walk-through with the evening staff. They always left together no later than 7:15 p.m. There was a daily journal kept up in the office, and it was full of notations from opening or closing staff and miscellaneous notes regarding light bulbs, supply shortages, suspicious characters hanging around, etc. Nothing was too trivial or petty to be noted. This was a Raven and Simone thing: "Document, document, document!" and Simone was the queen of documentation.

Outside, the investigation into this homicide was in full motion. The CSU team would run the prints through the crime lab and would wait more patiently than the lead detective. They wanted to get this body to the morgue and on a table before giving the investigators any formal information.

Simone told the truth: "We haven't had any real problems with anyone. But…" She caught herself, but it was too late.

Asher sat straight up in his seat and put his hand on Simone's. He asked, "But what?"

Simone took a deep breath and told the detective, "A few months ago, we were getting threatening phone calls from the ex-husband of one of the owners, then he started showing up here, making a scene every time he came in. Sometimes he'd show up drunk at around four in the afternoon. We had to call the police several times. There is a restraining order. But even that wouldn't stop him!" Simone continued after a pause, and her voice was steady as she pulled her hand away from Asher's and put both hands in her lap. "A month ago, he was here, screaming profanities at all of us. I got between him and Lacey. He said horrible things to her. He swung at me with his fist and missed. I screamed at him, 'Get out! If I call the police, you're going to jail, and if you ever come in here again, you'll be very sorry. You'll be dead and sorry!' But those were just words so he would leave."

In tears now, Simone didn't try to hide her face. She was the woman who had always stood up for the underdog. What Mason Asher didn't know was if she had ever threatened anyone before that or if she hated bullies. Pierce was a bully trying to intimidate everyone at A Tasty Dish to a point just short of stalking. He wanted Lacey back in a bad way. He couldn't stand the fact that with the help and support of her friends, she had moved on with her life. He no longer had control over her. The power she had given him when he was busy wining and dining with her, sending flowers, and rapidly charming his way into her heart and her wallet was gone. Everyone warned her that it was too much too soon; they had said, "Lacey, girl, he comes on way too strong! Something just doesn't feel right."

It was just Lacey being Lacey as she dismissed the pleas of her friends. Everything they said to her fell on deaf ears.

Simone described to Mason the incident in February. "Pierce had beaten Lacey pretty badly and raped her! She called me to come pick her up. When I arrived to take her to my home, I turned around, and Pierce slammed the door. And he was on me before I could react. He grabbed me by the throat, started choking me, and pulled a switchblade on me. After that, Lacey and I both filed for a restraining order." Simone then added, "His full name is Pierce Samuel Williams."

Mason's brain was in overdrive as he remembered the initials PSW engraved on the gold watch the victim was wearing. The detective thought that he possibly had the identity of his victim. Though not able to show it, he was elated.

It was a busy morning all around. There was a homicide for West Division, and the sun had barely peaked over the scenery to the east; a long day was anticipated for law enforcement. This was not how anyone wanted to start their day.

The city's first body of the day was a white male, possibly late forties to early fifties, tall, with an athletic build. John Doe, now known as Pierce Samuel Williams on the west side, had taken two bullets up close and personal. The kill shot went straight to the heart from, best guess, a 9 mm. Someone knew what they were doing, and they wanted Pierce dead!

The detective assumed that Mr. Williams saw it coming and more than likely knew his killer. He had possibly been lured to the café for whatever reason, considering there was an order of no contact. Mason immediately thought of Lacey as a suspect; she was the ex-wife who was being stalked and harassed and who had been held for hours, raped, and beaten. Tortured by knowledge, he could decide at that time to end her life. But after being interviewed by uniformed officers as well as talking to her himself, Lacey's alibi was solid and confirmed. She had every reason to do this; however, following the facts, she was crossed off the list of suspects.

Mason, good at reading people, felt Lacey did not have it in her to shoot Pierce. Her husband had made her life absolutely miserable, and she had divorced him and chosen to move on with her life. He did not sense that kind of animosity toward her ex.

In fact, the entire staff, the management, the owners, and the daily patrons were cleared. No one tested positive for GSR (gunshot residue) or Pierce's DNA. Now Mason had to find out more about his victim. Maybe then he would discover a motive. It was evident to the detective that no one had anything kind to say about Williams, but surely, he did not deserve to meet his end in this manner.

Pierce Samuel Williams was described by all who dealt with him, including coworkers, as *a womanizer, a user, a condescending cokehead, abusive, mean, short-tempered, and self-important.* Mason interrupted his own thoughts as if to say, "Okay, I got it. He wasn't a nice guy!" But who hated him this much? Someone out there thought they were doing the world a favor. From looking at the scene, he could tell that this was a definite ambush. Whoever pulled the trigger got very close, less than two feet from Pierce.

Alibis and Investigations

No GSR (gunshot residue) was found on anyone, and there was no DNA other than the victim's. The persons-of-interest list was dwindling; all individuals interviewed had solid, verifiable alibis. Lacey, the ex-wife, was tending a bar and actually worked a double shift that night when another bartender called in sick. Chloe was meeting with the CPA at her home, going through an annual audit of ATD's accounting records. Felicity was teaching a dance class of fourteen students; Raven was teaching her twice-weekly journalism class of twenty at the technical college; and Simone was in her warm-water aerobics class at the gym, verified by seventeen witnesses including the security camera. Plus, she had to sign in as well as out.

As for the men, Andre, Dietrich, Drake, Kennedy, Sebastian, and Walker met for beers and dinner and were shooting pool at Elm Street Billiards for their monthly boys' night out. They had done this for years, with a rotation of who picked the activity. This night, Diego did not join them because he was with Gracie and the girls at the ER from 7:30 p.m. well until after one in the morning, when they returned home exhausted. Six-year-old Skye had hurt her arm after school; she played around with schoolmates while waiting for the bus, and she tripped and fell on a raised slab of concrete on the sidewalk. Skye extended her left arm to catch herself, and there was a cracking sound. The only thing the child was sure of was that it was very painful and that she had never felt anything like it!

She cried initially from the pain, but Skye was a trooper. Once at home, she barely was able to do homework, and it was a struggle to get through dinner with her family. She constantly cradled her left arm, so Diego and Gracie took her to the emergency room. He sent a text message to Walker at 6:55 p.m. saying that he would not make the boys' night out because they were taking Skye to the ER.

Skye was discharged at one-forty-five in the morning, and Diego and his wife finally packed up two really sleepy girls to return home. Skye's arm was wrapped well, although she would have to see her regular pediatrician later to have it hard-casted. They were home for the rest of the night, which was also verified by the discharge sheet and several neighbors.

Pierce Samuel Williams was not a popular guy. Arrogant and smug, he physically abused his wife regularly. Then she divorced him, and that was that. It was evident to all who knew them both that he hadn't moved on. "Nobody leaves Pierce." He did not handle rejection well. But the ex-wife was cleared. Who would benefit from his death? By all accounts, no one and everyone. One thing for sure was that Asher had come to the startling conclusion that Pierce knew and trusted his killer.

Every question led to more questions with few answers, if any. His killer wanted to make a point and needed Pierce to see his ending. Why was he at A Tasty Dish after closing with a no-contact order in effect? That was the million-dollar question.

Asher was able to get a subpoena for Pierce's cell phone records. PSW had been a very busy boy! There were calls to the café every day, all throughout the day. They were short two-to-four-minute calls, maybe even five. Was he placing an order for food to have someone pick it up? Was he just harassing Lacey and the staff? Who was he talking to? Still, there were no incoming calls to his cell phone from ATD. What was the purpose of making these calls? There were more questions for the detective.

The phone records for everyone who worked at the café came under suspicion. All staff phone records came back, clearing each individual from having contact with Pierce. Detective Mason Asher desperately needed a break. This case was getting under his skin. What piece of this puzzle was he missing?

The investigative team tried hard to follow the evidence, but it's hard when there is not much to go on. Pierce had $200 and a change in his checking account, maybe one hundred in savings—nothing like the big success he made himself out to be. Pierce fabricated every aspect of his life. He was a fraud! They found one life insurance policy for $50,000. through his job, with his sister as the sole beneficiary. Investments? They found nothing.

When Mason spoke to Pierce's girlfriend, Courtney Napier, who had a startling resemblance to a twenty-something version of Lacey, the detective thought, *Are you kidding me?* Courtney was interviewed in the tiny, cramped, one-bedroom apartment she and Pierce shared. The top cop discovered while waiting for Courtney to get him a glass of water that all the bills sitting on the table were in Courtney's name. He found that very odd.

Courtney spoke to Mason openly and, in a few minutes, said, "Pierce was coming in to some money! Somebody owed him some money, and he said he had to meet this person at that coffee place, A Dish or something like that. I really don't know." Mason asked Courtney if she knew how much money Pierce was getting paid. She blurted out, "Fifty large. I mean, $50,000!" She giggled, not that anything about this was funny.

The detective believed that now perhaps he had a money trail to try and follow. Every good cop knows you always follow the money.

It was discovered that after the divorce, Lacey had sent Pierce a cashier's check for $30,000 with a note typed in the memo section at the bottom saying, "Leave-Me-Alone Money." He managed to burn through that in a couple of months, then started to either call, show up, or text for more. Lacey had been his meal ticket, and maybe if he had treated her better, he would've been on this side of the dirt. Pierce was a bum but now a dead bum! That transaction was traced through Lacey's bank. Pierce deposited that into his bank four days later, and his party started.

Pierce always bragged to anyone who would listen, "I know people in low places, people from the wrong side of the tracks! You don't ever want to get on my bad side." To pretty much all who knew him, his bad side was his only side. He dabbled in cocaine when he could afford it, and he always had a dose of Xanax or some other narcotics on him. Perhaps these unsavory, illegal habits had something to do with his demise. Maybe he had tried to outsmart or double-cross the so-called heavy hitters he claimed to know.

Mason Asher could find no one—not coworkers, not the one sibling that he had contact with, and not even his ex-wife—that was sorry that he was no longer among the living. His own sister could not recall to the detective one fond memory or express any decent sentiment toward her brother. The folks at A Tasty Dish (staff as well as regular patrons) seemed to echo in agreement, "I never thought too much of that man or at least not as much as he thought of himself!"

The detective had a team review the phone logs over and over again with no luck. Looking for a $50,000 transaction from all accounts at ATD should have been easy. Nothing! The medical examiner did note that Pierce had fine black nylon fibers on the inside of his hands. Was he paid? Did he get the money? Was that how he was lured to the rear of the café?

Mason was getting frustrated, exhausting leads that were leading nowhere and to no one. He returned to the crime scene many times and just couldn't figure it out.

If this was an inside job, surely, the guilty party should have slipped up by now. Not that it mattered, but everyone had passed the polygraph tests, with not one person raising eyebrows on deception.

As for Pierce's car, it had been taken to the vehicle crime lab for a good going-over. Even though they could find no other DNA except that belonging to the owner, no other person's fingerprints were there either and no blood spatter—more nothing. The victim, they concluded, was not attacked in his vehicle. It seemed as though he was at the back lot of the café on his own. Where on earth were the nylon fibers from?

The detective was puzzled, confused, and getting angry. This was a feeling Mason Asher was not used to, and he didn't like it one bit! At times, he sat at his desk, cursing under his breath, wondering what he was not seeing clearly. What could be hiding in plain sight?

They made contact with some of the people in "low" places, the usual suspects that their victim made mention of at a time or two.

These were people who sold drugs, people from the so-called wrong side of town that would do anything for money. A few characters familiar with Pierce admitted to selling him product, but as with everyone else so far, alibis were checked and verified. With no new witnesses, no new evidence, and no new forensics, eventually, the homicide case went cold.

Not a day went by that Mason Asher didn't think about that particular case.

The thing about Pierce was that he should have realized that as much as he bragged about being a big fish in a big pond, in reality, he was more of a guppy. There's always a bigger fish! As connected as he tried to convince everyone he was, how could he not understand that other people have connections too? For Pierce and his self-serving attitude, it could have been very easy to be outsmarted and out-maneuvered by someone he saw as no threat, especially a woman. According to the late Mr. Williams, "they're too stupid! All they can do is wait for a man to come around and tell 'em what do!"

Moving On

We've got to live no matter how many skies have fallen.
—D. H. Lawrence, *Lady Chatterley's Lover*

In the days, weeks, months, and years that followed, no one ever mentioned the unpleasantness that was the existence of Pierce Samuel Williams, not that anyone bothered to ever speak ill of the dead. It was just easier to move on and dismiss the negative effects he had on the lives of all the people he touched.

ATD was now busier than ever, and every Saturday morning after eight, you had to wait to be seated. Business was booming! On holidays, if you wanted A Tasty Dish dessert for home, you had to have your order placed before the cut-off date, which was two weeks prior. On Christmas Eve, the café closed at 4:00 p.m., and it closed on Christmas Day. Large $20 cheesecakes with special holiday flavors including the flavors Baileys Irish Cream, eggnog, peppermint, cookies and cream, and caramel apple and cheesecake by the slice in the shop sold out every day!

In November, they offered large pumpkin, sweet potato, and apple pies as well as peach cobbler, and everyone wanted one or two. Some ordered one of each. The assembly lines worked well in putting these together, and the staff was paid overtime. Easter was different; it was cheesecake time again, and just like all other holidays including Valentine's Day, the assembly lines buzzed along. ATD was in a flurry, and they couldn't wait for the days to end. Despite the achy feet, sore muscles, tired hands, and laughter, it was hard work, but it was fun! The time together as a team was priceless!

The owners at ATD were doing well professionally and in their personal lives. Everyone was thriving. Chloe was ecstatic that Dakota was accepted into an accelerated nursing program. She was doing well, just like Tallulah, Reese, and Mia; and their parents, of course, were proud that they had taught their offspring how to maneuver through life. Stressing the importance of hard work, focus, and sheer determination had served them well. The girls had turned into bright young women right before their eyes, and scared as they were, each of them was beginning to realize that the dreams they had could come true!

Dakota would be home for a brief break before her intense eighteen-month program at the University of Arizona. She was excited, proud, and very nervous. She was advised by her counselor that "about three hundred nursing students will start the program. Maybe one hundred will complete the classes and graduate. Most can't handle the demanding pace, and some don't handle stress well. This program will test everything about you and show you what you're really made of." Dakota was ready. She would approach this just as she had everything else that mattered in her life: head-on and deliberately. No one could stop her. They had all been told when they were very young, "Don't ever let anyone tell you what you can't do!"

The owners all had their schedules to cover the café, and they all had other activities that they were passionate about as well. Each had a family, which was priority number one. With Dakota at U of A, Chloe ran her marathons, and her quilting had become a rather lucrative side business. She did her shifts at the café and continued to do all the accounting for ATD.

Since Mia left for school in New York, Felicity had her dance classes, which she was teaching on Tuesdays, Thursdays, and Sundays. Plus, her sales in crafts and wedding planning services were doing quite well. Felicity and Simone still worked together on menu rotation and new items at ATD.

Lacey put in more time at the café, working evenings. She dropped the part-time jobs, enrolled herself in two classes at the university, and became a very strong advocate for the local domestic abuse hotline. After Pierce's homicide, Lacey transformed herself.

The stunning beauty no longer displayed the insecurities that let her fall victim to the likes of men like her ex-husbands. She no longer wore clothes that were too tight or too low-cut, which she had done at the request of men who would eventually take advantage of her good nature. Lacey was out of her shell, and she was marvelous, a force to be reckoned with! She was smart, and she decided to use her brain instead of her looks. Besides, it hadn't really served her well.

Raven busied herself while Reese was at Brown University by submitting her screenplays. She had written one that a major network was interested in kicking off as a pilot for a sitcom. Also, she was still teaching creative writing two nights a week at one of the local colleges. She along with everyone else worked as a team to market ATD, and Raven still controlled all things related to human resources.

Simone was working on another novel, taking her warm-water aerobics three times a week. She worked hard to make the most of ATD, and there was talk of opening another location somewhere between Madison and Milwaukee. She still found time to volunteer for causes that hit close to her heart.

Simone had played matchmaker with Lacey and Mason at one of her BBQs. The two had been dating for a while, and by all appearances, it was getting serious. Now Lacey knew truly what it felt like *to be treated like a queen*! All of her friends agreed that Mason was her knight in shining armor.

Help Is a Friend Indeed

A couple of years passed, and no one ever mentioned Pierce Samuel Williams. He was not even a bad memory. For everyone at A Tasty Dish, he had simply ceased to exist. He was gone and forgotten.

Dakota had graduated from her nursing program with honors, now a newlywed and happily employed at one of the hospitals near her new home in Madison. Tallulah was still in LA, working at JPL and coming home every chance she could, but they kept her plenty busy, though she made it home for all major holidays. Reese was settling in comfortably with her fiancé in their new place, six miles from Drake and Raven. Mia would be graduating from FIT soon, and her plans after that would be flexible until she secured employment. She was busy sending out her résumé.

In the cold case of the homicide victim Pierce Williams, Pierce never got his $50,000 pay. He had been celebrating all day, even taking cocaine from his dealer with an IOU, insisting that he was good for it. The one debt PSW always paid was to his dealer. The guy was no joke. If you owed him, you paid him. That was all there was to it! Failure to pay was nonnegotiable, and you did not want to be on the receiving end of noncompliance. The dealer was a businessman, and he had quality control people.

Yes, Pierce had been lured to A Tasty Dish, but they could never find the evidence as to why he was there. Although it was no secret, Pierce did a lot of his dirty dealings behind ATD, everything from procuring coke and other pharmaceuticals to hooking up with other women in cars. He was a snake in all his dealings.

He was promised money to stay away from ATD as well as anyone who worked there by none other than Simone. Fortunately, greedy is as greedy does. She sent him a legal form advising him that he could not share information regarding the payment with anyone, or he would forfeit the cash. He sent his electronic signature back through the burner phone. He was serious, and this was easy cash. He didn't have to work for it, which was how he preferred his cash. He felt the same when Lacey gave him $30,000 just to go away and leave her alone after their divorce.

Simone invited her old college roommate MacKenzie and her husband, Kyle, to come out for an extended weekend of rest and relaxation in Madison. They were Tallulah's godparents and actually got to see more of her than her parents did. She needed a courier to deliver the money to Pierce. She wanted someone neutral and knew the two could handle him easily.

When the time came, the money was placed in a regular nylon bag with a zipper at the top. MacKenzie would show him the cash, at which time he would give her the burner phone he had been using. Predictably, he'd insist she join him for a drink somewhere. Kyle was to wait in the car for fifteen minutes. He knew his wife could handle herself if Pierce got any wild ideas.

When MacKenzie arrived, Pierce was already there, standing in the shadows. She smiled to herself, thinking about what a pitiful, little man he was. He needed to beat women so he could feel powerful. She stood three feet from him and unzipped the bag. He smiled, and MacKenzie closed the zipper. The joke would be on him; there were fifties and hundreds on top, and underneath were all ones.

He turned for a moment, thinking he heard a noise; and when he turned back to face her, MacKenzie was standing there, holding a 9mm with a silencer attached. Pierce laughed and said, "Little girl, you trying to rob me?"

MacKenzie said, "I have a message for you from Simone. You were told you one day would put your hands on the wrong woman and that there'd be hell to pay. Today is the day you pay up!"

She dropped him where he stood. He didn't think this was real. He didn't think this was the end. Kyle walked in right on time.

Wearing gloves and painter's jumpsuits, they moved the dumpster to the door, with Pierce in between. They stopped and peeled off their jumpsuits once they were out of the area.

The flight departure for Kyle and MacKenzie was on time. They were flying from Milwaukee back to LAX bright and early on Tuesday morning. MacKenzie sent a FedEx to her office. They both had carry-on bags. This had been a hell of a business trip to help a friend take care of a problem.

The New Queen

All went well. All entities of A Tasty Dish were quite prosperous. The dessert orders alone during the holidays had become a monumental undertaking. They had to hire extra help for every holiday. They were still having fun, and the ladies finally had the chance to take time off. A Sunday-afternoon a spa day was a big reward for the hard work.

Lacey and Mason had taken several vacations together. This time they had gone to France. While there, a sheepish, boyish detective proposed. Thanks to Simone, Mason had gotten all the information he needed to plan the surprise for Lacey. Months later, the fierce five were planning Lacey and Mason's wedding. The shock to all was that Mason Asher was a very involved groom!

The couple wanted a small elegant wedding, family and very close friends only. They decided on having the ceremony and reception at the Edgewater Hotel, with a view of the lake. Mason fit in perfectly with the group, joining the men on their monthly *boys' night out.* The guys respected him as well as his career. He was a genuinely nice guy, but mostly, it was the way he treated Lacey. It didn't hurt that he was looking forward to retiring and spending time enjoying life with his new wife.

He was kind to her and spoiled her a little. He loved her. She had never felt appreciated by men; and they all watched as Lacey, after she started dating Mason, transformed into an incredibly strong woman. She finished school at the university with a degree in business and took on a more leadership-oriented role at ATD. Lacey knew she was loved. Mason playfully nicknamed her Baroness, and now she loved being treated like a queen!

About the Author

Regi Jackson-Rotar grew up as the youngest member of a military family. Traveling the world at an early age, she developed a sense of adventure with a level of curiosity to match. Regi is a retired executive assistant in the sports and entertainment industry and has spent much of her time as an active volunteer in the medical community. Now that life has changed its pace, she and her husband enjoy living in Wisconsin.

In her writing, Regi loves bringing strong, diverse female characters to life and showing us the bonds of friendship that last a lifetime.